SANCTUARY

ZONE CYBORGS BOOK 4

JESSICA MARTING

SHADOW PRESS

SANCTUARY

Sanctuary (Zone Cyborgs, #4)

ISBN 978-1-989780-17-6

Cover design by German Creative

CONTENT WARNING:

This book contains discussion of abuse; surgery is shown on the page.

For David

CHAPTER 1

IT WAS the worst possible time to find himself stunned into immobility, but Captain Jason Formosa couldn't force his feet to move. All he could do was stare at his rescuer.

This was the captain of the *Gray Ghost*, Cecily Barris? *This* was the mercenary who would save him and the rest of his cyborg brothers-in-arms?

She was smaller than he expected her to be, but he knew her appearance had to be deceptive. A few wisps of dark hair had escaped her gray cap and mask, and even if they hadn't, there was no way not to notice the feminine body encased in her fitted, matching flight suit.

In his shock, he'd forgotten that he could barely speak, his voice silenced by his captor's horrifying cybernetic enhancements. He tried to express his surprise at seeing what his rescuer looked like in the flesh, but all he could manage was mouthing the words, "What the hell?"

Before she could retort, Danvers and Ralston collapsed on either side of him. An uncharacteristic wave of nausea roiled through Jason at the sickening sound of their bodies crashing to the floor, and he didn't need to utilize his sensors to know they were dead.

All eight of the silenced cyborgs on the Omega-Three-Omega base had shared an illicit broadcast link, the only way they could communicate with each other without their jailer knowing. Dr. Garrett Jacoby would have had all of them killed or worse had he known about that link. But sharing it made their deaths that much worse to him. He'd physically felt their bodies dying, and he hadn't been prepared for that.

He swayed in place, emotions he'd been batting down for years threatening to overtake him. This was the worst possible time for them to return.

The *Gray Ghost*'s captain slapped at his arm. "Move!" she snapped. "I'm on a deadline right now and I still have someone else to rescue." She stepped over Danvers's body as he was nothing more than a puddle on a city street, moving down the corridor that led to the room nicknamed the Oasis. Another cyborg had been kept in the giant water tank there since before Jason ended up on Oh-Three-Oh.

"Who?" Jason tried to say, mouth forming the word. He was the one who'd sent out the SOS when he snagged a link to the galactic net.

He could sense the irritation rolling off her in waves, but she still answered him. "My brother's in there," she said, pointing down the corridor toward the Oasis. "The one who's been a mermaid all this time. Now let's find that Jacoby guy and let me kill him."

Eight months later

Jason didn't know gorkian trees could produce so many leaves, nor that they constantly shed. He was sure he could spend all day, every day, just raking up leaves on the small farm he'd found himself on since he arrived in the Brava System. His employers and housemates, Valenna Merchant and

Anders Barris, had repeatedly apologized for sticking him with the boring task, but Jason didn't mind.

The gorkian's star-shaped leaves were pretty, for one thing. And their colors changed depending on the amount of rain the farm received. More rain meant bright blue and green leaves; less, a more subtle yellow-green shade. But Kurkay-2, the border planet he now found himself on, always had some amount of rain in its forecast. Jason didn't mind that, either. It was peaceful here. He needed peacefulness right now.

He collected a large pile of blue leaves in a bag that would later be mulched for the vegetable garden Valenna had planted directly at the back of the small farmhouse. They were almost too lovely to destroy, he mused as he hefted the bag over his shoulder.

The ear comm Anders gave him his first day on the farm trilled, breaking him out of thoughts. He jumped in surprise, nearly dropping the bag. He quickly tapped it to reply. "Hey."

"Sorry to bother you," Anders said. "But we have a visitor."

There was a note of distaste in his voice as he said the word 'visitor,' and Jason couldn't help but smile a little. He had a pretty good idea who it was, and he didn't share Anders's opinion about her. "Is it Cecily?" he asked.

"Yeah. She says she wants to talk to us and it's important."

"I'll be at the house in a few minutes," Jason said. There was no point in refusing to see Cecily Barris, Anders's younger sister, not that he really wanted to. Despite Anders's misgivings about her, Jason still found her intriguing. Seeing a visitor, especially her, was better than being alone.

It felt like he was always alone since he finally managed to escape Omega-Three-Omega's cyborg project. His family hadn't exactly been thrilled to see him again. He thought they might at least be interested to know he was alive, but he was wrong. They would've preferred him dead rather than a cyborg.

We're your family now, Valenna had assured him when he asked for a place to stay over six months ago. *You're welcome to stay with us as long as you like.*

Jason wanted to believe that, he really did. Valenna had insisted that family didn't earn their keep, but he wanted to help out around their farm startup and feel useful again.

He could've used his enhanced state to his advantage and returned to the house that much faster, but walked at a normal pace instead, pretending he was still normal. It was so easy to do that here.

He patted the head of Dolly, the farm's resident goat who'd wandered over to him. Then he left the bag of leaves beside the turned-over patch of ground where Valenna was expanding her garden and let himself into the house. Anders nodded at him, his expression a little pinched as it always was when his sister showed up.

Cecily herself was lazily sprawled across the secondhand couch in the living room, gray flight suit impeccable, her expression cool and unreadable. Valenna sat opposite her, a total contrast in her patched-up trousers and braided hair with wisps escaping. A smear of dirt marred her cheek from working in her garden.

Jason sighed a little, then nodded at their guest. "Captain Barris."

"Just Cecily," she said and straightened. She gave him a small smile, and his heart twitched a little at the sight, damn it.

It must be the enhancements acting up.

She was smart, resourceful, and beautiful, and all of that made it easy to forget what she was.

She was a stone-cold killer, the polar opposite of who she'd been before she received a life-saving cybernetic heart, no longer the person Anders remembered before he let himself become a cyborg. He'd done that to save her.

Even though she'd helped save him and the other cyborgs on Oh-Three-Oh, Anders couldn't keep himself from hating her at how cold she was, or be appalled at what he considered her total lack of conscience. She hadn't cared that Danvers, Ralston, and later Bell had died. While Jason still found her fascinating, her lack of care about their deaths rankled him, too.

Damn his stupid self for noticing that tiny smile forming on her full lips. *Damn it.*

"What do you want?" Jason asked, not wanting to bother with niceties.

"I'm here because I need your help," Cecily said. She looked around the room, at the three of them assembled there. "Any of you will do, but preferably Jason," she added.

"Could you be a little more specific?" Jason asked.

"Well, Anders and Valenna are still in their honeymoon phase," Cecily said, like he was an idiot. And he might very well be. Of course, they wouldn't want to leave their farm right now. "And they bought this place only a few months ago. They're still working on it."

"Jason's working on it, too," said Valenna firmly. "We're happy to have him here."

"Just cut the shit and tell us what's going on," said Anders, visibly irritated.

"You know, you used to be happy to see me," said Cecily, clearly affronted.

"Yeah, that was before you started killing people," Anders shot back.

She narrowed her eyes at him. "That's a small part of my job description. I already told you that."

"But you still kill people."

"Only the ones who deserve it," Cecily said. "And I'd like

to remind you that *you* were ready to kill Garrett Jacoby back on Oh-Three-Oh." Anders opened his mouth to speak, but Cecily continued. "Those are the kinds of people I kill. Now, I need some help, and like I said, preferably Jason."

"Why me?" Jason asked.

"Because you're the cyborg closest to where I was when I found out some very important information related to your cybernetics, and you were a captain in the military, which means you're smart," Cecily said. "And your having this info is literally a matter of your life or death. Remember when I filched everything from Jacoby's lab?"

Everyone nodded.

"I turned it over to my client who hired me for it," Cecily said. "Most of it encrypted, and a lot of it has only been decrypted recently. And one of those encrypted files stated that some of you guys—the quiet ones—have kill switches built into your cybernetics." Her dark eyes met Jason's. "You're one of them."

A strange numbness spread through him at that bit of news, and Jason had to sit down. The reminder that he'd been forcibly silenced by Garrett Jacoby still had him shaking whenever he thought of those years without his voice. The revelation that Jacoby might be able to still harm him from beyond the grave actually managed to shock him. Cecily's news had him fumbling for words, and it took a few seconds for him to speak. "How do I disable it?" he asked.

"That's just it," Cecily said. "The only way it can be deactivated is if we find someone who worked for the original cybernetics company Jacoby worked at. I have the name of a former doctor who worked on the Zone's project who lives here now. He defected to the Brava System after his cybernetics research company was dismantled, right around the time of the first conflict." She paused, maybe for dramatic effect. "It's Dr. Marshall Caron himself."

"So, he's been here for around fifteen years," Jason translated. "And does he still work in cybernetics? Because none of us have had good experiences with people who did their own off-the-books research. Oh, and it's the *actual* Caron we're after?"

"From what I've been able to uncover, he seems like a good guy," Cecily said.

"Good by your standards or ours?" asked Anders.

"Both," she said. "Honorable doctor, worked on the border during the war, and it seems like he stopped working in cybernetics after he shut down his research facility."

There had been other former Caron employees who continued their monstrous research after Caron Cybernetics was closed, and Jason tried to convey that in the look he shot her way.

But if he had a kill switch in him... "Can you elaborate on this switch?" he asked.

"Jacoby built it into you," Cecily said. "I'm not sure where. He had the power to kill you at will, which is what happened with your friends back on Oh-Three-Oh."

Jason closed his eyes at the mention of Danvers and Ralston, and later, aboard the *Gray Ghost*, Bell. The memory of their bodies dropping to the floor, those heavy, final thuds, still woke him up in the middle of the night.

"And does someone hold, I don't know, a kill switch controller we don't know of?" Jason asked. "Because if there's no one out there controlling the switch, I don't see the point in drawing attention to its existence or undergoing more surgery."

"I wouldn't be here if that was the case," Cecily said. "That kill switch in your head—or heart, or wherever it is—is designed to fail. That's why it has to come out." She stood up, stretching her legs. "There's also an issue with my new heart, similar to your problem. So, we both need to find this doctor and have ourselves repaired. I need you to come with me in case I die in space and my ship needs to be piloted. I got a hell of a deal on the *Gray Ghost*, but she still wasn't cheap."

Jason exchanged glances with Anders and Valenna. He didn't need to be on the same broadcast link to know that Anders thought he should go with his sister. "What about the other survivors?" he asked. "Have you contacted them about the kill switches?"

"You, Danvers, Bell, Ralston, and Alexander were the ones with them according to your blueprints," Cecily said.

Blueprints. Like he was a shuttlecraft instead of a man. Anger and shame seeped into him, the same emotions that always came to surface when he thought about his cybernetic state.

Jason didn't want to leave the farm and his quiet days of sweeping leaves. He didn't want to leave Kurkay-2's spectacular sunrises and sunsets, the planet's soft rain that fell every afternoon or the rainbows that followed them, or Dolly the goat. He didn't want to leave Anders and Valenna, the only friends he had now. But if the kill switch malfunctioned, he'd leave them, anyway. At least if he went with Cecily, he might have a chance of returning. "All right," he said. "I'll go with you. How long do you think this'll take?"

"We still have to find the doctor," she said, just as Anders asked, "Are you sure about this?"

"How hard could that be?" He knew Cecily had a remarkable skill set; he'd seen it in action.

She hesitated half a second too long. "The last I heard he was living on Sidra Prime," Cecily said. "On the other side of the System."

She was hiding something else, Jason knew that for sure. She was going to pull him into her plans without giving him the full picture. Just like Garrett Jacoby had when he offered him tens of thousands worth of scrip for his participation in what he claimed was a tiny medical experiment. Jason would be stronger, Jacoby said. Smarter. Harder to kill. Few of those promises turned out to be true.

Jason thought about Kurkay-2's sunsets and his life here. Going with Cecily was likely his only chance at survival and seeing those sunsets again.

"So, are you coming with me?" Cecily asked.

Jason nodded. "Yeah."

Anders immediately pounced on Cecily as soon as Jason left the living room to pack. At least she was expecting him to be pissed off this time.

"What's really going on?" he demanded.

"Just as I told you," she said, affronted. "I'm trying to be helpful, but you don't seem to appreciate that these days."

Her mind flashed back to the night eight months ago, when she coordinated a rescue effort with the captain of the *Ensign* to retrieve the ten people Garrett Jacoby held under his control on an abandoned military installation. The *Ensign* was there solely to pick up Valenna Merchant, and Cecily found out later that she'd fought back against her rescuers, one of whom was her sister, Cressida. Cecily was there for the others, and to steal as much information about the Zone military's former cyborg program as possible for her client.

Anders went along with the information theft, and she even let him talk her into going to Echo-7 to pick up Valenna after the rescue. It wasn't until a couple of days after Valenna joined them that everything really went to hell.

She brushed those thoughts aside. Anders seemed determined to be difficult and unwilling to acknowledge how much Cecily was forced to change since he volunteered to be Jacoby's merman cyborg.

"What Jason needs is specialized surgery from someone who knows cyborgs," she said. "There aren't a lot of people out there anymore with that knowledge." The only two people who'd illicitly continued cybernetic experimentations—Garrett Jacoby and Colton Byers—were dead. Cecily's hopes were pinned on Dr. Marshall Caron, the founder of the defunct Caron Cybernetics, and living on Sidra Prime. Cecily would be able to find him eventually, but she wanted help. A cybernetically enhanced mind would be a valuable asset in her search.

Jason Formosa needed the kill switch removed; Cecily needed to replace her cybernetic heart. She'd been living on borrowed time since she had her transplant five years ago.

But Anders surprised her. "I know," he said, actually sounding close to agreeable. "I just don't like to see him uprooted again when he's finally living a stable life. Things didn't go that well when he tried to reunite with his family."

But just as soon as he said those words, Anders clammed up, like he realized he shouldn't have spoken about Jason's family. That just made Jason a little more interesting to Cecily. What had happened after she dropped him off on Renza eight months ago?

At least they'd have something to talk about during their trek for Dr. Caron.

Jason reappeared in the living room, duffel over his shoulder. "Ready to go?" he asked.

"That was quick," said Cecily.

"Yeah, well, the sooner we go, the sooner I can come back," he replied. "I don't have that much stuff, either."

Anders and Valenna rose from their seats, offering hugs and goodbyes. Cecily had to focus on the rainy landscape through the window to give them some privacy.

I wish Anders still said goodbye to me like that.

"You'll definitely come back," said Valenna, wiping away tears.

"I plan to," said Jason, but there wasn't much conviction in his voice.

Idiot. He was traveling with Cecily Barris, the Gray Ghost herself. Of course, he was going to return.

He was dry-eyed when he switched his gaze to settle on Cecily, and for some stupid reason, her cybernetic heart did another little flip-flop. It had to be a sign of its impending failure and not the result of looking at his sad, dark eyes.

"Ready to go?" he asked her.

She took a second to collect herself before replying, "Yes."

CHAPTER 2

THE *GRAY GHOST* was a repurposed luxury transport that originally belonged to a Zone-based billionaire who lost everything when his company folded. It still bore the original high-end finishes and sumptuous cabins, but it had also been retrofitted with a top-of-the-line weapons array, including masking that hid their heat signatures and a rudimentary cloaking device. Cecily rarely used that one, preferring to change her ship's ident codes to avoid detection instead.

She couldn't help but preen a little when she led Jason past its airlock accessway to the main corridor and he muttered, "Hot damn." She looked down at the deep pile maroon carpet muffling the deck, still in pristine condition, and silver-flocked paper covering the walls. It was the same decor the ship had when she rescued everyone from Omega-Three-Omega eight months prior.

"You've seen this before," she pointed out.

"I was in the hold," he replied. "We all were. Easiest way to spread out and think about what had just happened."

"Oh." She remembered their hurried flight from the frozen planet, how she'd essentially tossed all the surviving cyborgs in one of the converted holds. Only Anders bothered with wandering the ship to find her, to plead for a stop to Echo-7 for Valenna.

"It's nice, isn't it?" she continued. "Let me show you to a cabin and then we'll go."

"About that." Jason caught up to her as she strode down the corridor to the ship's aft where the cabins were located. "Where exactly are we going?"

"I told you Marshall Caron is on Sidra Prime," she said. "I'm not sure where, exactly."

"That doesn't exactly bode well for us, you know?" Jason said.

Cecily ignored that remark and unlocked the door to the cabin next to hers to let him in. It wasn't as large, but it was still beautifully appointed, and she was pleased at Jason's sharp intake of breath when he took in the room's furnishings. "He defected to the Brava System around the first conflict," she said. "He volunteered on the frontlines and when he aged out of the military, took off. I'll be able to find him eventually, but I'd like the help and if I happen to die before we can get to him, you'll need to take care of the *Ghost*."

"As beautiful as this ship's interior is, I still hope nothing happens to you." Jason perched on the end of the bed, testing the mattress.

It was an offhand remark, spoken by someone who probably didn't like her that much, but Cecily still liked it.

"And I have to say that this wasn't what I was expecting," he continued.

"I can't go around stealing secrets in a garbage scow, can I?" she asked.

Jason pointed to the cabin's attached bathroom. "I bet that's a water shower in there, too. I guess water makes it easier to wash off the blood when you kill someone."

"Are you actually put out that I killed Jacoby?" she asked. "Because he deserved it."

Jason surprised her. "Sorry," he said. "I'm not angry about you doing that. I think you showed him too much mercy. I would've made his death as painful as possible." He looked like he wanted to say something else, but changed his mind. "I'm still dealing with everything that happened," he finally added.

"Got it." She turned away. "I'll be on the bridge, taking off, if you need me. Don't worry about strapping in, it'll be a smooth ascent."

———

Jason was still taking in the state of his cabin when the *Gray Ghost*'s engines rumbled to life. *Don't strap in, my ass.* He looked around the room for a place to tie himself to and came up lacking.

Had he and the rest of the rescued cyborgs been strapped in the last time he was aboard the *Gray Ghost*? He was sure of it. He remembered the jumpseats they'd all been strapped into.

His enhanced brain immediately brought up the memories of takeoff. How smooth it had been. At the time, he thought he'd been hallucinating it, or his cybernetics were doing something to maintain his equilibrium.

He just couldn't remember what it was like last time.

There must be an emergency jumpseat *somewhere* in this cabin. He'd have to ask Cecily about that.

He finally took a seat on an overstuffed armchair in the corner opposite the bed, noting that it was at least bolted down. He gripped its arms as the *Gray Ghost* began her ascent, but the ship's trajectory didn't follow the pattern he was used to. It felt like the ship levitated, staying level as it rose in the air.

Huh. Jason stood up as the *Ghost* flew faster upward, and while he noticed some subtle changes in the ship's gravity controls, he could still move around freely. He remembered his earlier words when he saw the ship's carpeted corridor, how he hadn't meant to let that "hot damn" escape him, but those words again ran through his mind.

He left the cabin and returned to the corridor, looking for the bridge. He found it a deck below, just as luxurious as everything else he'd seen so far: red and black-papered walls, spotless red-framed control panels, and a holo display, currently showing a rotating Kurkay-2 perched between the red velvet-upholstered pilot's and co-pilot's seats. Splayed back in the pilot's seat was Cecily, a navigation panel in front of her, long legs crossed at the ankle on the red-carpeted floor. She looked deceptively relaxed as she navigated the ship through the planet's atmosphere.

Without turning her head to face him, she said, "What do you think of the lift-off?"

"I'm not going to lie, I was looking for a jumpseat."

"This ship used to move Zone movers and shakers," she said. "The well-heeled in this part of the galaxy don't like to be inconvenienced by something as trivial as strapping in for launches and landings. Can you imagine how pissed off a billionaire's daughter would be if she had to get out of bed because of heavy air?"

"I guess not." Without asking, Jason sat down next to her.

To his surprise, she didn't protest. Instead, she tapped at the navigation panel in front of her and the heavy air engines roared to life. He was bounced around a little as the ship broke Kurkay-2's atmosphere, but they were far gentler than he was used to. He was pleasantly surprised at the ease with which the ship launched herself into deep space.

The heavy air engine immediately quieted. The vibrations under his feet almost ceased. Jason would have worried about that had Cecily not been so calm.

"It isn't the red velvet seats that make this an amazing ride," he said.

"No, but they're a nice touch, aren't they?" Cecily keyed in a few commands on the navigation panel, then swung it away from her and stood up.

"I can't say I've ever been on a bridge like this. Or a ship like this, for that matter."

"I like to travel in comfort," she said.

Jason had been living with Anders and Valenna long enough to know that Anders had grown up orphaned from a fairly young age and enlisted as soon as he could to help provide for Cecily. His sister's taste for the finer things in life hadn't come from her background.

Red velvet seats. What the actual fuck? "Did you decorate the place?" he couldn't help but ask.

"No, it was already like this when it came into my possession," she replied. "I didn't see the point in changing things. Plus, velvet feels nice."

She had him there, but he'd be damned if he was going to admit it.

"You still haven't told me where we're going," he said. "Sidra Prime's a big planet."

She actually looked irritated at that remark. "I said we have to do some research first."

"We couldn't have done that on Kurkay-2?"

"And get bitched at by my brother? No, thank you."

"You know he cares about you," Jason ground out.

"All he does, whenever we see each other, is get pissed off about what I do for a living and lecture me," Cecily replied. "I'm not expecting him to fall down at my feet in gratitude for helping him off Omega-Three-Omega, but it would be nice if he'd stop going on about what I had to do to survive. It could've been worse."

The flippancy with which she spoke about her only remaining family member rankled at him. Jason refrained from responding to that, knowing that if he did, he might explode at her, and they'd only been in each other's company for a short time. If she was going to be the last person he saw before his kill switch malfunctioned, he wanted to keep the peace as much as possible.

The *Gray Ghost* wasn't big enough to contain two angry people with proverbial axes to grind.

He recalled his disastrous reunion with his family on Renza. His parents hadn't been thrilled to find out what he'd been turned into, and it was just easier for everyone for him to leave, never to return.

He couldn't tell if she was waiting for a response, but he said, "I guess so."

Cecily set a course for the biggest public spaceport on the opposite end of the Brava System, close to their shared border with the Parradin Quadrant, and left the bridge. The journey to Sidra Prime would take a couple of days, and she had almost nothing to do until they arrived.

Dr. Marshall Caron seemed to have fallen off the edge of the universe since he retired from medicine and the military. She could try conducting more research on him, but she already knew the endeavor would be pointless.

Which meant she was alone with her thoughts, most of which revolved around her failing heart. Her *second* failing heart. Somehow, this time around was scarier than the first.

She leaned against the corridor wall outside the bridge and closed her eyes. She felt a tension headache coming on whenever she thought of her impending heart failure and massaged her temples in an attempt to stave it off.

It wasn't just her heart. It was Anders's rejection of her, too.

He'd done what he had to do to stay alive. Why was he such a jerk about her doing the same thing?

"Hey."

Jason's voice snapped her out of her thoughts, and she straightened. "What's up?"

He pointed at the end of the corridor. "I don't know where anything is. I was hoping to get something to eat."

"Oh." She so seldom had visitors aboard the *Gray Ghost* that she'd forgotten her manners. "Sorry. The lounge is one deck below." She led him to the stairwell, down a flight of steps to what had once been the entertainment deck, and she thought she could feel his eyes on her back. She couldn't say she would mind it if he did.

This deck boasted a lounge-galley combination and a sim chamber that Cecily used as a gym. "Feel free to check that out," she said, thumbing at the sim chamber's door. "The programs came with the ship and I never bothered to update them when I acquired it, but there are plenty to choose from."

The lounge's lights cycled on at their entrance, revealing a black-and-white striped tiled deck, huge viewports that offered a view of the starscape beyond, and gleaming black fixtures. A newly installed top of the line replicator and food processor dominated most of one wall.

Cecily expected Jason to mumble another appreciative phrase, but instead, he said, "What do you mean by 'acquire'?"

"No one died for the *Gray Ghost*," she said. "The menu isn't huge, but the nutritional components are the best of the best, and there are ready-meals in the processor cabinet if you'd rather that."

"Could you answer the question, please?"

It was the "please" that did her in. Cecily motioned to a pair of deck-locked chairs arranged around a small, black-lacquered table. Jason sat down. "The honest answer is I bought it below market value," she said. "The guy who sold it to me filed for bankruptcy and ran into some serious legal troubles. Want a drink?"

"What kind?"

"Tea, coffee, I think I have some wine around here, too."

He surprised her again when he replied, "Wine, please."

"You got it." She found an unopened bottle of red from an exclusive winery on Garshan and poured two glasses. She took the seat across from Jason, the space between them small enough that their knees touched.

Jason raised his glass to his lips, then paused. "Are you sure we should be drinking if we have ticking time bombs in our bodies?"

Cecily had conducted enough diag scans on herself in the *Ghost*'s sickbay to know the current state of her cybernetic heart, but she'd never considered the possible effects alcohol might have on it. She paused for a few seconds, considering a lie to tell him about her health, but knew it would be pointless. He wasn't a stupid man; he'd figure it out, sooner or later.

It was important that Jason trusted her.

"I don't know," she said slowly. "I don't see how it could hurt. You haven't had a drink since I sprung you from Omega-Three-Omega?"

"My family doesn't drink at all, and neither do Anders or Valenna." Now it was his turn to consider his words. "No, I haven't."

Anders had never been much of a drinker and Valenna was in substance recovery, so their keeping a dry house made sense.

"You don't drink much, either," said Jason.

"I don't like drinking alone."

"Good policy." He raised his glass, and she clinked hers against it.

"What are we toasting to?" she asked.

He shrugged. "I don't know. That we don't die, whether it's due to faulty cybernetics or killing each other."

Cecily didn't know if he'd intended to say something that would make her laugh, but it worked. The anxiety she'd been secretly harboring since she found out about the kill switch and her impending heart failure evaporated enough so she giggled, and she set aside her drink.

It might not be so bad, traveling across the Brava System with Jason Formosa.

CHAPTER 3

WHEN HE REALIZED a glass of wine probably wouldn't activate his kill switch, Jason let himself relax a little. He even felt himself warming up to Cecily; after all, she was in the same situation as he was.

Both of us built with faulty body parts.

Which reminded him … "Can I take a look at my specs?" he asked. "You *do* have them on board, right?"

Cecily looked at him like he was an idiot. "No," she said. "I'm trying to track down the doctor who could save our lives and I don't have our blueprints."

His burgeoning friendliness toward her evaporated. "I'd really appreciate it if you weren't sarcastic," he said.

She drained her glass and set it down on the table with a bang that was louder than necessary. "Of course, I do," she said. "I should show you where the sickbay is, anyway."

Jason quickly finished his wine, and she put both glasses into the wall-mounted recycler before leaving the lounge.

The *Ghost*'s sickbay was one deck below them, and like the rest of the ship, had all the trappings of luxury, at least from Jason's unpracticed eye. The single diag bed looked more advanced than what had been in Garrett Jacoby's lab on

Omega-Three-Omega, as did the rest of the equipment. It was smaller than he expected, and he doubted the room could hold more than two people. As it was, it was a tight fit for him and Cecily.

Just as it was at the table in the lounge. For such a luxurious ship, there really wasn't a lot of space in the common areas.

Cecily activated a holo display next to the diag bed. An image of a man was superimposed above the display and slowly rotated. It took Jason a few seconds to realize he was looking at an image of his own body: faceless and featureless, save for highlighted parts where he'd been enhanced. He recognized the scars on his hip from an old friendly fire accident when he was in basic training and the ports in his neck and wrists that Jacoby removed shortly after installing them. The rudimentary ports had left ghastly scars, even by Jason's standards.

Anger rose in him, bright and hot as a flame, as he watched the rotating image. He forced it down and said evenly, "This is the first time I've seen anything like this."

"You never wondered what was done to you, exactly?" Cecily asked. She activated a visualizer screen and reams of information about his cybernetics scrolled past, all of which he could easily follow with his ocular enhancements.

"I could've run a complete diagnostic on myself," he said. "But it didn't occur to me do so after we left Oh-Three-Oh. I wanted to be normal, you know?"

"And you never picked up the kill switch?"

"I wouldn't know what to look for." Jason's education, like most soldiers, was limited to whatever public schooling was available on their home planets, followed by basic training. "A lot of these terms and numbers mean nothing to me."

Except his larynx. It had taken only a couple of days for his voice to fully return, although eight months after the fact, it was still a little hoarse and scratchy. He suspected it always would be.

Cecily expanded the image with two fingers and pointed out a few features. "Here's where your medulla was enhanced, for increased adrenaline production," she said. "And in your cerebellum, Jacoby did..."

But Jason wasn't looking at his cerebellum or anything else on his body's image. Cecily's voice faded away as he stared at it, finally seeing what was in front of him. The red and blue veins and arteries paled in comparison to the shiny silver-colored metallic components that had been inserted into his body, threatening to overtake whatever scraps of flesh and blood he still had. He felt himself swaying on his feet, and nausea rose in his throat, but his systems overrode his anxiety about the picture in front of him, and he could only remain rooted to the deck, unwillingly transfixed.

"Jason."

He shook himself out of his stupor, finally making eye contact with Cecily. She looked uncharacteristically concerned as her eyes searched his face. "Jason?" she repeated. "Are you okay?"

It took a few seconds for him to form an answer, and for a horrifying moment, he thought he'd lost his voice again. "Yeah," he finally managed, his voice a croak. "This is hard for me to see," he said, gesturing to the holo display's image. "I knew what was done to me, but..." He trailed off, unable to put what he was thinking and feeling into words. "I'm sorry," he said. "I don't mean to make this weird."

But Cecily surprised him again when she spoke. "Don't apologize. I had no idea," she said, her voice uncharacteristically soft. "I didn't even think about flashbacks or trauma. I'm sorry."

Neither had Jason. Until Cecily had shown up on her brother's homestead, he'd been content to while away the rest of his life in obscurity, collecting leaves for mulch and maybe raising some farm animals on Kurkay-2. He'd never expected to see his own cyborg body's blueprint, nor had he really wanted to.

He remembered Cecily's frantic collection of information before the *Gray Ghost* took off from Oh-Three-Oh, how she scrambled around the base. She was collecting all that stuff for her client, she'd said, and she clammed up as soon as the cyborg survivors were crammed on to her ship. After that, the only words spoken were between her and Anders as he argued that they needed to stop on Echo-7 to collect Valenna.

Anders had finally exploded on Cecily, telling her that he was worried about Valenna's sobriety should she stay in her home city. Cecily had tersely informed him that she needed to return to the Brava System as soon as possible and Anders could go to Center City on his own time if finding Valenna was so important to him. In the end, Anders talked his sister into making that stop, certain that Valenna would be willing to uproot herself immediately and start her life over in a whole other system. He'd been right; according to Anders, he hadn't even needed to coax her into leaving her sister behind. The *Ghost* had spent less than an hour at a cheap public spaceport in Center City.

There was one more mystery about Oh-Three-Oh that Jason hadn't solved yet. "Who were you working for?" he asked suddenly. "When you came to Omega-Three-Omega for us? Anders never told me who it was."

"That's because I didn't tell him."

"So, who is it?" Jason forced himself to look away from the holo display and look Cecily straight in the eye, willing her to answer truthfully.

She looked away for a few seconds, then changed the holo display image to show a different figure. Even if the female image wasn't a regular human save for the glowing orb in its chest, Jason thought he would have recognized it as Cecily anyway. He knew that shape, he even liked it, and he shouldn't.

"I got your distress call," she finally said after a pause.

Jason remembered that clearly. He and the other cyborgs who weren't kept in a water tank had managed to circumvent their programming enough to create the mental link they all shared, undetected by Jacoby. When they'd been ordered outside the base to conduct repairs following a power outage, Jason was able to connect to the galactic net and put out an SOS. The *Gray Ghost* had immediately responded and promised to be there with help in a few hours.

"That doesn't answer my question," he replied.

Cecily fidgeted with a visualizer, stalling. "I'm not going to be mad," he said, hoping that wouldn't be a lie. "But I've been jerked around for years thanks to these stupid enhancements. I'd really appreciate it if someone could just tell me the fucking truth about what's happened to my body, okay?" His voice cracked on that last word, and he could tell by the shift in her expression that she'd picked that up.

But beyond that, he couldn't tell what she was thinking.

"I *know* you got my distress call," he continued. "I'm right here, aren't I? And Anders and Valenna are still on Kurkay-2. Who were you working for?"

Even Anders, when Jason pressed him about Cecily's intentions, didn't know and seemed to have given up on getting an answer out of her. Or maybe he just didn't want to deal with Cecily any more than he did.

Cecily was silent for another moment, gathering her thoughts, he supposed. "Originally, I was hired by a guy who wanted as much data about cybernetics as possible," she said. "He didn't have any connections to Caron or the Zone military, nothing like that. I agreed to the job since I was looking for Anders anyway. He knew I had a cybernetic heart, and I guess people with my skill set aren't always open about that." She sighed. "Anyway, after I agreed to the contract and got enough money from him to keep searching, I found out he wanted all that data for the wrong reasons."

Jason closed his eyes, knowing what she was going to say next and what she'd likely done after.

"He was going to sell it to the highest bidder," she said. "He knew the data could be manipulated to create a breed of cyborg slaves, essentially. By then I'd already taken his money and had a pretty good idea of where to look for Anders, so I arranged for an accident to happen right as I landed on Omega-Three-Omega."

"Of course, he had an accident." Jason didn't know how to process that information. Even as an enlisted grunt in a war zone, he doubted he was directly responsible for as many people as Cecily had killed.

"The fuel line on his shuttle blew," she said. "Poof."

Jason expected that kind of answer, but it still shook him a little. She didn't even look remorseful.

Would he have felt bad about killing a guy who wanted to continue Jacoby's work? He had been ready to kill Jacoby. He'd been fantasizing about it since the day the mad doctor took away his voice and physical will.

But he was trying to move past that, trying to put that part of his life behind him, including his time in the military. He'd been truly content to collect leaves on Anders and Valenna's property, keeping to himself.

"Are you *sure* your employer was the only person looking for cyborg data?" he finally asked.

Cecily hesitated a half-second too long for his liking.

"God damn it," Jason said. Desolation washed over him, the likes of which he hadn't felt since his days in Jacoby's grasp. "I'm never going to be just be allowed to live my life, am I? I'm going to spend the rest of it looking over my shoulder, wondering if some fucking bounty hunter is going to come after me or a kill switch in my body decides to flip." He would have punched something to further drive his point home, but he wasn't entirely sure that Cecily wouldn't have jettisoned him into open space should something happen to her ship.

But she surprised him. "I'm pretty sure no one else is after that data," she said. "Well, I *hope* no one else is. The person who hired me only heard rumors, and I didn't tell him what I knew or suspected, and he never saw the information I found on Oh-Three-Oh. I've kept that encrypted. No one knows for sure who the successful cyborgs are, let alone where they are. It's a big galaxy."

Jason knew now that he was one of several success stories, or as close to success as possible. The only acknowledged successful Caron Cybernetics subject lived in relative obscurity on Echo-7 in the Zone, partnered with Valenna's older sister. Like Jason, Anders, and the rest of the survivors from Oh-Three-Oh, he'd eventually rebelled against the people who modified him.

"I also needed that data for myself," Cecily said. "The person who did my surgery wasn't entirely forthcoming about what he'd done, and as a patient, I had a right to know what was installed in my body."

Installed. Like she was a machine.

Before Jason could ask her further about that and everything else related to their journey, she said, "Now, it's my turn to ask you questions. I know you went back to your home world after we left Oh-Three-Oh. Why did you leave again?"

At the mention of his family, Jason felt himself blanch.

Did she have other enhancements she wasn't sharing with him? Or was she just trying to get a rise out of him, piss him off enough so he wouldn't press her on her mercenary past?

He resisted the urge to tell her to fuck off, that it was none of her business, but instead, he said, "My return wasn't taken that well."

"I would've thought they would be delighted to see their long-lost son again."

"Yeah, well, you thought wrong." Jason cleared his throat and moved past her to the sickbay's door, his arm brushing against hers as he did so. A frisson of heat raced along his skin at the contact, which he ignored.

It was simply being in close proximity to a woman for the first time in years, that's all.

He paused at the doorway. "Could you send a copy of all that to my cabin?" He gestured at the holo display.

She looked confused, but she nodded. "Yeah, no problem."

"Thank you." He turned around.

"Jason?"

Damn it. "Yes?"

"What else did I do wrong?"

It was such a stupid question that he would've laughed at her had they not been in open space with kill switches in their bodies, trying to find the one doctor who could help them but may as well have dropped off the face of civilization.

If he replied truthfully, that would just invite more conversation. So, Jason said, "Nothing."

Cecily left the sickbay a few minutes after Jason did, wanting to keep as much space between them as she could for now.

She'd fucked up. She knew that the minute she'd asked about his family, regretted the question as soon as it left her mouth. In the years since her heart transplant, she seemed to have lost her social skills. She hadn't had a meaningful conversation with someone since the last time she saw

Anders before he signed up for that ghastly cyborg experiment.

She made her way back to the bridge, not that there was much for her to do there. She rubbed her temples, feeling a tension headache coming on as memories came flooding back: the realization that Anders wasn't coming back in time to get her life-saving surgery. The desperation that led her to seek out a black market surgeon, the bargain she struck with him. He was the first person she killed.

For fuck's sake.

She was tired of killing people.

Cecily understood the allure of living on a simple homestead and planting a vegetable garden. Anders and Valenna enjoyed a level of freedom she never had, and she envied them for it.

She'd told herself after getting her new heart that she would finally be able to live for herself, and that hadn't happened. Hopefully, after she had another heart, a better one, she would finally get to live how she wanted.

She wasn't sure what she would do just yet, but she had the ship and enough funds to take her time to figure it out.

And maybe regain her social skills while she did so, too.

Jason stayed in his cabin for the rest of the day and evening, wondering just what the hell he'd gotten himself into. It was morning before he realized the easiest thing to do would be clear the air with Cecily, if for no other reason than he was getting lonely.

He shouldn't have bitten Cecily's head off for asking a simple question.

He should've known that seeing his anatomy superimposed on a holo display would bother him.

He should've told himself that the reason he reacted to Cecily as he did was because of his discomfort with her profession, not because she asked about his family. Most people he knew had loving families, no matter the size; Anders and Cecily had once been fiercely close, at least according to Anders. Hell, he'd agreed to become a cyborg for her.

He ran his hands over his face, thinking about how he was going to apologize to Cecily. Because she deserved that.

He stalked out of his cabin, wondering where to find her on a ship the size of the *Ghost*. On impulse, he said, "Computer?"

One of the corridor panels lit up. "Yes?" said a flat, masculine voice.

"Where's Cecily?"

"Cecily Barris is currently in the sim chamber," the comp replied. "Shall I open an intraship link for you to communicate with her?"

"Don't worry about it."

"Is that a negative?"

"Yeah. Thanks."

Jason retraced his steps until he found himself in front of the sim chamber, then paused, unsure what to do next. Did he just let himself in or alert Cecily somehow? He checked the doorway but couldn't find an alert system.

Before he could decide, the door opened for him. A wave of tropical heat hit him full in the face, and he crossed the threshold into a beach scene.

And Cecily, lying on simulated sand on her back in a black two-piece swimsuit, a drink in hand. "Hi," she said. "Come on in."

"What the hell?" Jason had spent his life on cold planets when he wasn't on a battlefield. He'd never been to a beach.

"Take a seat."

"There aren't any," he pointed out.

She was wearing oversized dark sunglasses, but he suspected she was rolling her eyes at him when she spoke. "I meant the ground."

His boots sank into the surprisingly soft ground when he walked in her direction, and he felt the fine grains shift underneath him when he sat down. He pointed at the water lapping at the beach. "If I touch that, will I get wet?"

"No. I was too cheap for that upgrade. I just like to lie in the sun." She crossed her bare legs at the ankle and drew a large sun hat over her face.

He may as well get his apology over with. "I'm sorry about earlier. I didn't mean to freak out on you."

She lifted up the brim of her hat just enough to expose her mouth. "Don't worry about it."

"No, I was rude and I didn't need to be. You don't know what happened with my family on my home planet. I could've just said I didn't want to talk about them and left it at that instead of flouncing away like a spoiled teenager."

She shrugged. "Okay, apology accepted."

Jason looked at the water, which looked far too clean and clear to him, but it wasn't like he'd spent any time around oceans. "What's this program based on?"

"An undiscovered gem in the Brava System," Cecily replied. "Burns Point on Sidra Prime. It's a luxury clothing-optional resort and a little out of my way, so I use the program instead." She paused for a second.

"I've never been to a beach."

"Neither have I, but I'd like to go to one someday. My brother would disagree with that, however."

Jason nodded, even though she couldn't see it. Anders refused to deal with any body of water deeper than a bathtub. "They don't believe in enhancements," he said bluntly.

She slipped the hat off her face and sat up. "What are you talking about?"

"My family. My parents. They don't believe in enhancements or even medical treatment that doesn't involve prayers. We're from Renza. Religion is big there."

"Oh." She slipped her sunglasses off her face, meeting his gaze. "So, after I left you on your home world ..."

"They said hello and offered hospitality because that's what their faith tells them, but I'm not one of them anymore." Pain lanced through him at the memory of his parents and siblings' stiff demeanor around him, the subtle hints and later orders that he needed to leave. "How familiar are you with the Great Faith of the Stars?"

She gave a small shrug of her shoulders, causing one of her swimsuit straps to slip off her shoulder a little. He tried not to notice it.

"Renzans follow the Great Faith," he continued. "Well, it's more their twisted version of it. It emphasizes nature over technology and twice-daily prayers to the stars. There isn't much in the way of hospitals there and no one wants them, anyway. My family probably would've disowned me if I broke my leg and had it splinted, let alone the cybernetics."

"Why did you do it in the first place?" she asked. "Agreeing to become a cyborg when it's against your religion."

"Financial security after I was supposed to be discharged from the military," Jason replied. "I wasn't super religious in the first place, and they weren't crazy about my enlisting."

"So, you took on a huge risk for financial gain, and for what?" she asked. "It sounds like your family wouldn't have accepted you either way."

"I already knew I wouldn't inherit anything," Jason said. "They run a very successful farming operation. My sisters will never want for anything, even if they don't find husbands, which they will. The Great Faith requires marriage of its adherents. Not the monks, though. The monks are the only ones who can do whatever they want."

Cecily wrinkled her nose and lay back down, putting her sunhat back over her face. "That sounds like a shitty religion. I'm glad you escaped from it."

"I still loved them," Jason replied.

"Yeah, I get that." But she sounded bored when she said the words. Apathetic. It bugged him.

He wanted to remind her that Anders loved her too, that his friend would have relished an opportunity to rebuild a relationship with her, but didn't. He was unsure how that would be received, and besides that, he'd already had a tantrum that day. There was no point in adding fuel to their already tenuous friendship.

He supposed they *were* friends, in a way, thrown together by circumstances and necessity. It wasn't that different from his military unit.

Jason was about to get up and leave, find somewhere else on the ship to mull over his life and feel sorry for himself, when Cecily said, "I think Anders and Valenna have the right idea, you know."

"Settling on a small planet in the Brava System and starting a farm?"

"I'm not crazy about the farm thing," she said. "Sorry. I'm not into dirt and animal shit. But living a quiet life—I'm ready to start doing that. I think I'd rather a city, though."

Before Jason could offer a response, the shrill of red alert klaxons rang through the sim chamber. The program immediately shut off, revealing thermowired walls and smooth control panels.

"Shit!" yelled Cecily. She leapt to her bare feet and bolted through the already-opening chamber door. "We have visitors!"

Jason followed her as she raced through the corridors, the emergency lights flashing red. "Incoming," said a monotonous comp voice. "Scout detected within *Gray*

Ghost's perimeter. Please proceed to the bridge as soon as possible."

They burst through the bridge's door and Cecily slid into the captain's seat. The forward viewscreen revealed nothing unusual until she tapped at the command console. An image of a small round, silver-colored ship filled the screen. A cheap, generic Scout ship, large enough to only hold one person. According to the data readout on the viewscreen, it was moving toward them at an aggressive speed, weapons array online.

"Who is it?" Jason asked.

"Damn it!" Cecily snarled at the screen. To Jason, she said, "How are you with traveling in subspace?"

"I—you know, I don't think how I feel about that matters right now." He'd never traveled through subspace.

"Sit here," she said, vacating the captain's seat. "I'm going to try something from navigation. Don't puke on my deck."

Jason considered making a smart-ass remark in response, but he might end up jettisoned if he did. He did as she ordered. "I'm a ground soldier," he said. "Just a heads-up."

"Press the red keys when I tell you to," she said from behind him. "I have an emergency course plotted."

"Where are we going?"

"We're getting away from that Scout," she said. "And I'll tell you who they are when we're safe."

The *Gray Ghost* lurched forward, then picked up so much speed the stars turned into a blur. The sight made Jason a little nauseous, and he looked down at the command console to center himself.

Highland Subspace Gate, the console read. *ETA thirty-six seconds.*

"This boat has a subspace engine?" he said, but he was drowned out by a roar.

That would be the subspace engine gearing up.

The *Gray Ghost* shook, vibrations from her engines so strong that Jason had to hang on to the console to keep himself from falling out of his seat. The ship nosedived, and behind him, he heard Cecily yelp, "Press the red keys!"

A bright, purple light flare coalesced on the viewscreen, and with a mighty groan, the ship was sucked into it.

CHAPTER 4

HOLY SHIT, *it worked! We're not blasted to pieces!*

Any triumph she felt over successfully entering the subspace gate was quickly forgotten when she tumbled to the deck from the impact in the most undignified manner possible. "Damn," she muttered, grabbing one of the comp panels for support to haul herself to her feet. Her *bare* feet, she remembered. In fact, now that the *Ghost* was safely in subspace and she could register temperature, the bridge's chill prickled at her mostly bare skin.

She'd deal with that in a few minutes. "How are you?" she asked Jason.

He stood up and stretched. "I could go the rest of my life without dealing with an emergency subspace entrance again. What the hell happened back there?"

Cecily double-checked the ship's reports to make sure her ship was the only one that made it through the gate. She breathed a sigh of relief at the confirmed all-clear before turning around to face Jason. "I'm trying really hard not to be sarcastic," she said.

"Yeah, I get we were chased into this," he said. "Could you be more specific?"

"That ship was a Scout," she said.

He cocked his head, waiting for an explanation before she remembered he'd been a ground soldier. "I know what a Scout is," he replied.

"They're often used by gray market contractors," she said. "Like me."

"I'm not going to pretend what you do is gray market," he replied.

"You don't have to. But contrary to what my brother's told you, I'm not completely immoral. My methods are a little unorthodox, but I don't kill innocent people. I have reasons for taking the jobs I do."

"The Scout," Jason reminded her.

"I'm getting to it," she said. "That ship was looking for me. The *Ghost* picked up a hot weapons signature."

"I saw that."

"Whoever was piloting that ship was out to disable my ship," she said. "It had laser and ion cannons showing hot, but only the laser was trained on the *Ghost*. However," she stressed, "My comp system's telling me it wasn't set to destroy."

"So, whoever was in it wanted to immobilize your ship."

"Yeah," she said. "And then either tow it or force their way on board."

"We were still in open Bravan space!" Jason said. "None of that makes sense! Maybe out in the Zone, in the Rims..."

"This is a part of Bravan space that doesn't have a lot of patrols," Cecily said. "It's a smaller population here, so there's less need for them. And keep in mind that entire parts of the System were decimated during the war, just like the Zone." Her mind flashed back to the morning she dropped off Corporal Adam Johnston in Remensky Harbor on Gamma-10, his home planet, after the rescue from Oh-Three-Oh.

Gamma-10 had been destroyed in the war and would never fully recover in their lifetime.

"And they're short on military personnel, patrols, you name it," she continued. "Plus, it's not like a lot of ships travel here outside of subspace. My subspace engine was retrofitted for the *Ghost,* so it's old, which is why I'd planned to find Marshall Caron in realspace."

Jason paled. "You're saying we're aboard a ship with a crappy subspace engine?"

She shouldn't have let that slip out. If she didn't watch her tongue, she might accidentally tell him that she'd never actually piloted in subspace before. "It's not like it's going to blow," she said. "We're perfectly safe as long as we're here. We just can't connect to the galactic net or with any other ships."

"I love how you're saying that like it should be reassuring."

"I don't have any reasons for traveling in subspace," she said. "The engine's fine, it's just old."

"I'm surprised you didn't keep it in top shape. You have fucking velvet-covered seats on your bridge, but your subspace engine sucks."

"The velvet came with the ship."

Jason pinched the bridge of his nose between his fingers and closed his eyes. Gathering himself, Cecily guessed. She appreciated it. She didn't want their time together to be spent arguing.

Plus, she liked the velvet. It felt nice against her skin when she had to haul ass to the bridge from her sim chamber-created beach.

She looked down at her swimsuit. She should probably get changed.

"It's not just that," Jason said. "We're completely cut off from civilization as long as we're in subspace." His gaze fixed on hers and fought the urge to fidget under its intensity. "What if one of us gets sick?"

Their living on borrowed time had completely slipped her mind when she forced the *Ghost* through the subspace gate. "Fuck," she said softly.

"Yeah. Just so you know, I don't know how to bring a ship out of subspace. If something happens to you..." He held out his hands, waiting for her to fill in the gaps.

"You're fucked, I know."

"How long are we stuck here, anyway? And where do we exit? Will it take us closer to Marshall Caron's last known whereabouts, at least?"

None of those things had crossed Cecily's mind when she jerked the *Ghost* toward the Highland Gate. "Let me check," she said, turning around to the navigation panel.

"I have to be honest with you, Cecily. I'm a little concerned that you don't know the details of what part of subspace we're in."

She wanted to whip around and yell at him that she knew what she was doing, but she didn't strictly know what she was doing, and admitting it would only fuel more questions that she didn't have answers for yet. She keyed a command into the nav console to bring up all the *Ghost* had about the Highland Gate, then blanched when she read it.

"Oh, shit," she said before she could stop herself.

Jason's words were measured, but she still picked up the angry undercurrent in them. "That's the last possible thing someone wants to hear when they're in fucking subspace."

"Would you rather we get blown up or boarded by the Scout?" she snapped. "They don't give a shit about my heart or your kill switch."

That retort shut him up.

"Okay," she said, adjusting the console better so he could see it. "The gate exit is..." She cleared her throat. "Um, a lot of days away. Like, twelve."

She expected Jason would blow up at this news. Hell, she

wanted to. But being stuck in subspace was still leagues better than whatever the Scout had in store for the *Gray Ghost*.

But he surprised her. Mouth a thin line of frustration, he closed his eyes. When he opened them, they glowed, the bright blue a stark contrast to his usually dark pupils.

"Um," she said again. "Your eyes—are you okay?"

He blinked in surprise. "Oh, yeah."

"They're glowing."

"They do that sometimes. You said we're going to be in subspace for *twelve days*?"

"Unless I initiate an emergency exit," she said.

"You mean drop the ship out of subspace before we get to the gate exit proper."

She nodded. "Yeah."

"I doubt I need to be a pilot or captain to understand just how fucking dangerous that has to be."

"Less dangerous than the illegal weapons array that was trained on us." The Scout had enough firepower on board to blow a hole through the *Ghost*'s hull. She wanted to keep his attention on the Scout, away from her lack of experience in subspace. She'd never dropped out before on any ship. The very thought had beads of sweat popping up along her brow.

"What's the chance of our Scout friend waiting for us at the exit?"

"I don't know." She leaned against the nav console, frustration and fear welling up in her. "Maybe not that particular ship, but there could be someone waiting for us at the exit. And I don't know how the subspace engine is going to play with the weapons array if we're exiting hot." She wanted to scream. Had she just prolonged a future encounter, if not their deaths, with whoever was piloting that Scout?

He must have picked up her frustration because his voice was a little gentler. "Can you find out if they followed us through the gate?"

"I can't," she said. "We're completely incommunicado while we're in subspace."

He was quiet for a moment, thinking. So was she, but for once she wasn't mulling over her options.

Anxiety clawed at her instead, the depth of which she hadn't experienced in years. Not since she found out her original heart was failing, and Anders volunteered to be turned into a cyborg to raise the funds to buy her a new one.

But thinking about those dark days brought back her memories of when Anders may as well have dropped off the edge of the galaxy. Panic splashed over her, but her steely determination to survive hadn't come to the surface yet. Cecily hated being weak, feeling weak, especially in front of other people.

She *was* weak. She could drop dead at any minute.

"Cecily?"

She blinked, trying to clear away her maudlin thoughts. "Yeah?"

He pointed behind her. "You just kind of zoned out and your comp boards are beeping."

The bridge's transmit file beeped steadily, and she silenced it with a fingertip. She opened the file and some of her anxiety eased. "I guess that filter was a worthwhile investment," she murmured.

"What?"

"It isn't totally legal."

"I'd be surprised if it was *any* kind of legal," Jason said. "What is it?"

"It's a filter that scans and picks up hostiles' information," she said. "Incoming and outgoing mail, comp systems information, that kind of thing. I bought a copy on the black market. Rumor has it the designer helped out in the galactic net's creation, but I have no way of verifying that."

"So, it's a hacking program."

"Yeah." Despite the terror rising in her at what lay ahead of them and her worries about their health, what lay before her put some of her fears to rest. She opened the file and sent it to the bridge's holo display. Easier for both of them to read.

Some of the information was garbled, just broken lines of code and text, which meant that the filter wasn't perfect. But it still managed to pick up a document, one that Cecily guessed was the Scout's instructions.

The ship was definitely looking for her.

Jason Formosa also being on board was just a bonus.

Jason stared at the information superimposed before him, shock holding him in place.

"I'm going to get dressed and then we'll talk about this," Cecily said.

"You don't want to talk about this *now*?"

She actually rolled her eyes at that question. "We're in subspace," she pointed out. "No one can communicate with us, no one can track us, and even if they could, good luck to them if they try firing on the *Ghost*. There's never been a successful battle in subspace, ever."

"That we know of," Jason muttered. The stars only knew how many times history had been rewritten by the Zone's government. Cyborgs weren't supposed to exist after Lukas Best's transformation, but he and the others rescued from Omega-Three-Omega were living proof to the contrary.

Cecily didn't offer a retort and instead left the bridge. "I'll be right back," she called over her shoulder.

Jason watched her retreating figure, a small part of him a little disappointed that she was getting changed.

Do not *start thinking about her that way, if only for the fact that either of us could be dead any second, she's Anders's sister,* he told himself. *And it's not like we're friends, anyway, even though I was trying, sort of. At least until the Scout showed up.*

He mulled over that until Cecily returned in a loose gray flight suit devoid of ship ID patches. "So, that Scout was looking for us," she reiterated. "Me, specifically. And they knew you're on board." Her fingers caught a piece of superimposed text and enlarged it. Jason's name, rank, and military ID number were displayed.

He couldn't help but shudder a little. "I don't have a civilian ident chip," he said.

"I guessed you wouldn't, considering your home planet."

"It has to be my cybernetics."

"Yes. Specifically, that military ident chip is keyed to the kill switch in your head."

A wave of nausea crested over him. "The Scout pilot was going to kill me." In addition to the kill switch being faulty, now he had to worry about whoever had his military ident information and what they could do with it.

"Possibly," she said. "Although based on the rest of what's here, I'm not so sure."

Jason's eyes scanned more of the information in front of them, noting there was nothing there about actually killing him. "Oh. Maybe they wanted to experiment on me before killing me."

Cecily didn't reply right away, her eyes glued to the information in front of her instead. "They were looking for me," she said. "You're being aboard is lucky for them."

Jason forced himself to look away from her, noting and hating that pinched, worried expression on her face, and back to the holo display. Its text scrolled past, slower than what he was used to thanks to his ocular enhancements but still at Cecily's speed. It meant they saw the most damning part of the report at the same time.

"They're looking for Marshall Caron," he said, just as Cecily muttered, "Shit."

"They're also after the Omega-Three-Omega research," she said. "And all of that is on this ship."

"We *have* to find Dr. Caron," said Jason. "And not just because of our health issues."

"They have a head start," Cecily said. Her jaw clenched and her hands formed fists before she took a deep breath, fighting for control over her temper. "God fucking damn it, I should've fought back. I should've at least sent a neutralizer to their defense shields before I panicked and forced us through the Highland gate. We have to find out who they're working for."

Jason looked back at the superimposed text. "It says 'WIFT.' Any idea of what that stands for?"

"Not a clue."

"It isn't military, at least."

Some tension eased from her posture at Jason's observation. "Oh?"

"That'll mean less firepower on their end," he added. "If that Scout was military, it would've locked on to the *Ghost* with a tractor beam or just blew her up."

"And then sifted through the rubble," Cecily said. "Yeah, you're right." She leaned against the nav console. "I still don't know what we're going to do about the subspace situation." Meeting Jason's gaze, she said, "Sorry, but I'm used to working alone. And I'm used to not fucking up a mission like this. I should've fought back."

"But what if you did?" he pressed. "And then lost the fight? Marshall Caron would still be in danger. The research you have onboard would have been stolen. Plus, we were in a civilian area. It wasn't that busy, but there was definitely traffic nearby."

"I know," said Cecily.

"You don't like to bring innocent people into what you do," he said.

"I said, I know." Her voice was a little sharper. "And again, you're right about all of that. Knowing how my luck was going, someone would've tried to help out or sent out a quadrant-wide Vessel Under Attack advisory."

"And then the military would've shown up."

"Someone would've," she said. "And it could've been made public, and every one of you cyborgs would have a target on your heads." Once again, she balled up her fists. "Fuck!"

She shut off the holo display. "I need to think," she said. "Figure out what I'm going to do next." She stalked off the bridge before Jason could say anything more, leaving him alone again.

CHAPTER 5

THE MEMORY of Cecily's first few terrifying days alone after Anders dropped off the edge of the galaxy came back came rushing back at her with all the force of the sim chamber's hurricane program. Not wanting to run into Jason just yet and tell him that she didn't know what she was doing in subspace, she stayed in her cabin, watching the time while away on the wall-mounted thincomp.

Once again, she was terrified and her heart was failing.

It was now past one in the morning, but she was too wired to sleep. All she could do was focus on the starless, bluish-purple void of subspace whizzing past her cabin's viewports. The sight only reinforced the pickle she and Jason found themselves in, all because she hadn't stayed in realspace long enough to fight back against the Scout.

She remembered how her energy was drained almost as soon as she woke up in those days years ago, an ever-present reminder that she was dying, how much effort it took to get out of bed and fetch a glass of water. And later, when she realized Anders wasn't returning, how she'd sought out a black market surgeon for help. She'd had to find the surgeon through a two-bit bounty hunter and mercenary based on Echo-7, a slimy fellow named Dalton who smirked too much.

Cecily forced the memory of the bounty hunter, the surgeon, and the whole procedure out of her mind, trying to think about the immediate problems at hand. She needed to force out the *Gray Ghost* back into realspace, and she had to save Marshall Caron, wherever he was. Only then would she let herself worry about her failing heart.

Plus, there was Jason to consider, too. They'd both been through a lot since acquiring their cybernetics, but she was never tortured. She hadn't been experimented upon the way he was.

He'd been rejected by his family, his whole culture. He had no one. As much as she and Anders fought, both of them were still alive. His frustration and disappointment in her notwithstanding, she was fairly certain her brother still loved her. At least, she hoped he did.

And she was pushing Jason away.

Anxiety had eaten at her since she flounced off the bridge, unwilling to let Jason see her scared. She'd been on her own for so long, was accustomed to the independence she'd cultivated out of dire necessity, that she didn't know how to open up to someone anymore.

Anders used to think of her as a great listener, to the point of being an empath. Cecily hadn't been that person for a very long time. She wanted to be. She wanted to give up her mercenary business, start over the way Anders and Valenna were on their farm. Like Jason was.

He'd opened up to her, telling her about his family's rejection. He hadn't gone into great detail, but she saw the pain and loneliness there.

She saw herself reflected there and had to leave. If she didn't, she would've broken down and cried about what a mess she'd made of everything since she helped rescue everyone from Oh-Three-Oh.

She squared her shoulders and took a deep breath. She would apologize to Jason, explain her reservations about forcing the *Gray Ghost* out of subspace early, and ask his forgiveness for endangering their lives.

Would he be awake at this hour? "Crew check," she said, her voice activating the *Ghost*'s comp system.

"Two passengers aboard the *Gray Ghost*." The voice was male and a rich baritone; like all the ship's over-the-top features, the comp's voice came with it, and Cecily didn't see the point in changing it. "Captain Cecily Barris and Jason Formosa."

"Is Jason still awake?" She didn't like to intrude on his privacy, but she didn't want to haul him out of bed, either.

"Yes, Captain. Ship's sensors indicate he is in the sim chamber."

She was a little heartened to hear that he was taking advantage of the *Ghost*'s amenities. "It's nice that it's getting used," she said.

"Please repeat your last command."

"It's nothing. Captain out."

The comp trilled an acknowledgement and Cecily left her cabin, making her way to the sim chamber.

Its doors opened automatically at her presence. The chamber was dark, illuminated by stars and a pair of twin moons. She was immediately suffused in a pleasant, dry heat, the smell of woodsmoke in the air. Sitting in the middle of the chamber, partially hidden by bushes and trees, was Jason, staring into a campfire.

"Hi," she said.

He looked up, the firelight reflected in his luminescent eyes. He blinked, and they looked normal again.

Something must have shifted in her expression at the sight, because he said, "Night vision is automatic."

She nodded. "Want some company?"

She didn't know she was holding her breath until he said, "Of course," and patted the space next to him.

Cecily plunked down in the dirt beside him. "I'm sorry about earlier."

He shrugged. "What for?"

"Everything."

"You know the Scout wasn't your fault, right?"

"Everything that happened *after* the Scout started chasing us was my fault."

"What else would you have done?" he countered. "You could've had us blown out of the space lanes instead or your ship stolen and the two of us murdered. You thought on your feet. I'm not mad."

"I'm sorry about stomping off the bridge and sulking in my cabin, too."

"Again, nothing to be sorry for."

Cecily wanted to scream. Instead, she snapped, "Why are you being so nice to me?"

He looked at her, incredulous, eyes glowing again. "Because I make a conscious effort not to be an asshole? Because we're dependent on each other right now? Holy shit, Cecily."

He looked like he was going to add something else, but closed his mouth, quiet again. "What?" she prodded. "I know you're not done."

Jason paused. "I respect Anders a lot. But I'm not him."

Cecily stilled, mulling over his words, realizing he was right.

She kept waiting for Jason to explode, to condemn her, to curse her out the way Anders had been since they took off from

Omega-Three-Omega, arguing about the dead cyborgs in her cargo hold. Then fighting over the side trips to Echo-7 for Valenna and dropping off Corporal Johnston on Gamma-10, a planet destroyed during the last major phase of the Zone-Brava System war, and the last one that left Rordan Alexander on Spaceport 44.

"Yeah," she said slowly. "You're not my brother. You don't hate me."

"Neither does Anders." His voice was uncharacteristically soft. "You've been apart for a few years when you used to be very close and were forced to adapt to your new circumstances. I don't think either of you understand the other anymore, is all."

Cecily felt tears prick at her eyes and blinked until they went away. "We were all each other had after our parents died."

"What happened, if you don't mind my asking? Anders never mentioned anything."

"It was an avalanche on our home planet. They were on a holiday in the mountains for their anniversary."

He paused. "Do you want to talk about it?" He sounded unsure.

She tried to keep her tone level, reminding herself that he was being nice. "I appreciate the offer, but no. It was a long time ago."

There was nothing to talk about that she hadn't discussed with Anders, that she hadn't mulled over in her mind a million times since their deaths when they were little more than kids. She'd stopped grieving for them a long time ago. She'd focused on her lost relationship with Anders over the last few months, instead, and her own possible impending death.

"I didn't plan for any of this," she said, keeping her eyes on the fire. "Not just the Scout chasing us through the subspace gate. My whole career choice."

"Well, yeah, I figured that. Most little kids don't decide they want to be a mercenary or assassin for hire when they grow up." Jason tossed a stick on the fire, making the flames pop. "That *is* what you do, right?"

"Technically, yes. Although I don't kill people at the rate Anders thinks I do. I mostly get information for the right price, but even now, I don't really do that." She had enough money socked away to keep her afloat for the rest of her life if she lived modestly.

But thinking about Anders, and sitting with Jason, reminded her of the night she helped rescue the cyborgs. It reminded her of the ones who didn't make it out, of Aaron Bell collapsing shortly after rescue. She knew now that his kill switch went off, and she was still haunted by the notion that she might have contributed to his early demise but had no way of knowing for sure.

She'd been initially resistant to bringing all of the bodies aboard the *Ghost* for burial, even though she'd had the equipment necessary to hold them, but she'd been too distracted by seeing Anders again to think that through. She was glad Anders and Valenna insisted on burying them in a private cemetery on their new home planet, if only to prevent someone from exhuming the bodies and performing obscene posthumous reverse engineering experiments on them.

"Did the other cyborgs who died have families?" she asked suddenly.

He shook his head. "No. Most of us didn't. I think that's why Jacoby picked us."

"How did he get you?" On second thought, she added, "If you don't mind talking about it."

"Not at all. I was on the frontline of one of the Bravan conflicts and got hit with friendly fire. It was a stupid accident and not the first time it happened, but I was laid up for a few weeks with a broken leg in a war zone with substandard medical facilities. Jacoby showed up one day, said he could get me a medical discharge, but I'd have to agree to enhancements for research purposes. The discharge and money he offered were enough to get me to sign up" He tossed another stick on the fire. "I should've known better, but he still lied to me. I was expecting to get better vision and strength."

"And you lost your voice."

"Yeah. I could whisper a little, but it pissed him off when I tried, so I didn't. I once tried to tell Valenna that when she first arrived at the base."

"Are you still mad? I'd be out for blood."

He looked at her like she was nuts. "You've already been out for blood. And for what it's worth, Anders isn't upset that you killed Jacoby. We were going to do that before you and the *Ensign* swooped in."

"I know. It's my profession that upsets him."

"And it's grief. You aren't the person he remembers."

Cecily knew that and hated it. "I can't be her anymore. I had to be this if I wanted to get my new heart and live."

"I get that. Anders will, too. Give him time."

"I don't know if I have that."

He put a proprietary hand on her arm, expression serious. "You do. You're going to get your new heart and we'll get my kill switch sorted out. We've come this far. We'll beat all this."

The small touch distracted her, and it took a few seconds for her to regain her focus. "Are you sure you're not religious?" she asked.

"No, just an optimist." Firmer, he added, "I need to be one right now."

He had a point. "All right. I'll try to be one, too." She shifted to face him, in more ways than physically. "I still don't know if I can break us out of subspace. I'm going to try because the alternative is being blown out of the lanes when we exit the gate. But I need you to know that I've never done it before."

"Have you checked the *Ghost*'s service logs?"

She nodded. "She's never been dropped out."

"You've gotten yourself out of tight spots before. How many things could go wrong?"

He really had no practical flight experience. It was scary, but his having faith in her was reassuring, even if it felt misplaced right now. She didn't know she needed that until now.

But a million things could still go wrong. He didn't appear to realize how many.

"A few," she said, parsing her words carefully. "But I promise, I will try my best to keep us alive long enough to get to Marshall Caron's hideout."

If she could find it.

One hurdle at a time. Get out of subspace, then find Caron. You can do this. Her inner pep talk didn't help much, but Jason's words did. "And thank you for believing in me," she said. "It's been a long time since anyone has."

He nodded. He closed his eyes, and when he opened them, they'd lost their luminescent glow. Trying to look more human, maybe.

Cecily didn't care. She liked them, powered-up or no.

His gaze was fixed on her in a way that sent a long-forgotten wave of heat roiling through her body, and she thought for a crazy moment he was going to kiss her.

She wanted him to.

She closed her eyes and leaned forward a few centimeters

...

But he stood up. "I should head to bed."

God damn it, she'd been way off. She followed suit, brushing sim chamber-generated dirt from her pants. "Yeah, I should get some rest, too." More brusquely than she intended, she said, "Good night."

The last words she heard as the chamber door clanged shut behind her was Jason ordering the program to stop.

I'm an idiot.

CHAPTER 6

CECILY WAS EATING breakfast in the lounge later that morning, not looking like someone who'd been awake in front of a simulated campfire just a few hours earlier. Jason hadn't slept much either, but he chalked much of that up to his cybernetics. He hadn't needed more than four or five hours a night since his enhancement surgeries.

He sat down opposite her, a cup of coffee in front of him. "Did you get some sleep?" he asked.

She shrugged noncommittally.

She was acting weird again, just like she had in the sim chamber. She'd clammed up and stalked away, and he'd spent the rest of the night wondering if he'd said something wrong.

"Is everything okay?" he tried.

"Are you serious?"

"I mean, is anything that I don't already know about off?" he asked. "I feel like there's this barrier between us that wasn't there before. Is it something I did?"

She shook her head. "No. It's just me."

There was something she wasn't telling him, but he wasn't going to press her on that. Not when they were the only two people aboard the *Gray Ghost* and someone was on their tail.

He changed the subject. "Have you thought more about dropping out the ship?"

"Yeah." She paused for a second, and he thought he saw doubt flicker across her face. "We should do it."

"I agree."

"But I thought about the other cyborg," she said. "Alexander, I think his name is?"

"Rordan Alexander, yeah."

"We have to find him," she said. "But I don't know who to track down first. We have to find Marshall Caron, but Alexander has the right to know he has something in his head that can kill him. And someone could already be after him anyway."

"So, you want to drop out earlier," Jason said.

She nodded. "As soon as possible." Another shadow crossed her features, and Jason's anxiety about their predicament increased.

She was definitely hiding something. Whether it was about the *Gray Ghost* or her expertise, he didn't know. But Cecily wasn't telling him everything.

"Can you get in touch with him?" Jason asked. "Once we get out of subspace?"

"I'll be able to access the galactic net and less well-known boards, so probably. He asked me to leave him on Spaceport 44 on the Zone side of the border after the rescue, and I did. I'm surprised that you don't have his contact information, actually."

"We didn't stay in touch. Alexander wanted to be alone." Of all the cyborgs on Omega-Three-Omega, Jason had known Rordan Alexander the least. He'd only been captive a year prior to their rescue and he kept to himself, rarely using their secret broadcast link to talk to the other men. He was an enigma then and now.

"So, that's one more thing we can't think about until

we're back in realspace." She got up from her spot at the table and fetched another cup of tea.

"Why don't we drop out now?" he asked.

She nearly dropped the cup. "I don't think it's safe yet, is all. The Scout's probably waiting for us to drop out earlier."

"It's been over a day." One more day that he had to live with a ticking time bomb in his head, one more day that she had the same in her chest.

Don't think about her chest, he told himself.

"Well, what do you want me to do?" She slammed her teacup down on the table. "Don't you think I know we're on a deadline? Do you really think I forgot about the utter fucking danger out there for both of us and for your friends and my brother?"

Shocked by her outburst, Jason leaned back in his seat.

"Cecily," he said calmly. "What is it you're not telling me?"

Was there something wrong with the *Ghost*? Were they condemned to spend the rest of their lives trapped in subspace, the ship eventually being spit out at an exit gate on the other side of the galaxy with their dead bodies aboard? Was that even how subspace worked?

He didn't need to use his enhancements to see she was flushed with anger, that her temperature might very well have risen. Except...

Her heart!

"I think you should check yourself out in the sickbay," he said.

"I thought you wanted to know what I'm not telling you."

"I know one of the things you're not telling me is that you're running a bit of a fever. You can tell me the other thing when we know what's caused it."

Her eyes widened in alarm and she touched her forehead. "I feel normal."

"You're not." He held up his hand. "May I?"

Wordlessly, she nodded, mouth a tight line.

Touching her forehead only confirmed what his sensors told him, and the gesture had the added effect of sending invisible sparks down his arm. "You're burning up."

"God damn it."

"Remember when we talked about what could happen if one of us got sick?"

"I know." She brushed his hand away. "I'll go to the sickbay. Want to come with? It'll be nice to have a second opinion."

"Because I'm a machine, too?"

She stiffened, and horror suffused her features, along with an alarming blush. "Oh, shit, Jason, no. I didn't mean it like that."

Did she? Jason wasn't going to argue with her on that, especially since it wasn't entirely untrue and he was worried about her health, first of all. "It's okay," he said evenly. "Let's go to the sickbay."

Why am I being such a bitch?

Cecily felt like crying again as she set up the sickbay's diag bed and lay down on it. On her direction, Jason activated the machine and keyed in the appropriate program.

She could have done it, but she liked it when he took care of her.

I like him entirely too much, and I'm treating him like shit because I can't tell him that I might have killed us both.

A chill overtook her when the diag bed cover was in place, and a cold sweat popped out along her brow. *Maybe I really am getting sick.*

A steady beep from the diag comp was the only noise in

the sickbay as it analyzed her body. "Pyrexia detected," the flat comp voice announced.

"No shit," muttered Jason. The remark drew a smile to Cecily's face.

"Patient's body temperature is one hundred and one point four degrees," the voice continued. "As the patient has a transplanted heart, medical assistance in an accredited hospital is recommended as soon as possible."

"Does she have an infection?" Jason asked.

Cecily understood the panic in his voice. She was feeling it, too.

"This sickbay's current available diagnostic technology has detected pyrexia."

"I mean, is her heart infected?"

"The current available diagnostic technology cannot diagnose if the pyrexia is a result of transplantation complications."

Before Jason could freak out further, Cecily said, "What is the recommended treatment?"

"Standard pyrexia treatment is recommended, which includes keeping the patient hydrated and warm and administration of fever-reducing pharmaceuticals."

"Is it contagious?" she asked.

"The detected pyrexia is not recognized as a known pandemic or epidemic infectious strain."

"That's enough," said Cecily, and activated the switch to remove the diag cover. Her head swam when she sat up.

"I've been sick before," she said to Jason. "Before and after my heart transplant, while I was on the *Ghost*."

"But not when you were in subspace."

"No. But I'm sure this'll pass." She tried to smile.

Jason clearly wasn't buying it. "Why don't you go back to bed, and then we'll talk about what to do next when you feel better?"

At least he didn't think she was at death's door just yet. "Do I really have a choice in the matter?"

"Of course. I just think you should listen to the diag comp and get your ass back in bed. I'll bring you some soup."

She slid off the diag bed and a wave of dizziness washed over her. For a second, she thought the ship tilted, but Jason remained unaffected.

"Want some help?" he asked.

She hesitated. He shouldn't be offering it when she'd bitten his head off and may well have killed them both. And she shouldn't be accepting his help.

But there was a softness in his metallic-tinged eyes that convinced her otherwise, something in them that said he was safe to lean on. And Cecily had been on her own for so long that the temptation to let someone look after her was irresistible.

"Okay," she said. "Thank you."

But instead of taking her elbow and keeping her steady, he picked her up in one smooth motion as if she was light as a feather and carried her out of the sickbay.

His own cybernetically enhanced heart remained strangely calm, beating at the rate it was supposed to, as he carried Cecily through the ship to her cabin. But that didn't mean that everything else in his body felt like it was rioting out of fright.

That fear wasn't for him, about what could or would happen to him should the unthinkable occur and he end up trapped in subspace, aboard a ship he had no idea how to pilot. If worse came to worst, he could download the ship's schematics and training materials into his head and figure things out.

It was all for Cecily, who he'd become more intrigued by during their time together on the *Gray Ghost* despite their squabbling. He'd only ever known her as the smart, independent, tough-as-nails mercenary, and he liked her.

He was probably the first person in her new life who knew the real Cecily Barris, who she'd evolved into.

Anders needed to get to know her, too.

He slid her cabin door aside and stepped into the cabin. As he settled Cecily on the unmade bed bolted to the deck, he noted that the cabin didn't hold the ostentatious trappings of the rest of the ship. It was luxurious but stripped down, decorated in neutrals. The wallpaper was peeling in a couple of places near the deck, which was littered with discarded clothes.

"You're messy," he said, then gently lay her down on the bed.

"You weren't supposed to know that."

"You've never let the mess creep out of your cabin?"

"I don't have enough stuff for it to leak out of here." Her voice was weaker, and Jason thought she might be even more flushed than before. "God, I'm cold."

Jason reached for the blankets bunched at the foot of the bed and draped them over her. His mind flashed back to his idea earlier about downloading everything he could about the ship into himself. He hated to bring it up now, but there was a possibility of the fever being serious.

He squeezed his eyes shut, trying to block out the images of Cecily's death from his mind. She couldn't die, not yet.

"What is it?" Cecily asked. "You look like you have something in your eye. Although I'm sure your ocular implants or whatever would force anything out."

He hesitated, trying to figure out how to phrase his idea and concerns without offending her.

"Tell me," she said. Despite her illness, she still managed to sound stern.

"Neither of us thought about this before," he began.

She raised her head, a little more alert. "I have, but I think I'm too sick to do anything about it now."

Mild alarm threaded through him. "What?"

Just as quickly, she leaned back against the pillows, and Jason thought her cheeks might have gotten even redder. "Nothing. Forget I said it."

He thought his heart might have actually done a little flip-flop at the possibilities her earlier words held. *I have, but I'm too sick to do anything about it now.*

His body, the traitorous thing it was, heated in a way that had nothing to do with a fever. "I can download everything about the ship into me," he said. "I don't know why I didn't think of it earlier."

"Because you don't like being a cyborg," Cecily said.

While Jason was open to having a conversation with her about the pros and cons of being a cyborg, this wasn't the time. But before he could explain that, she said, "You can access everything you need from here." She pressed a button on the nightstand next to the bed, and a wall panel slid away, revealing comp boards that matched the ones on the bridge.

Jason stared at them, unexpected shyness and embarrassment overtaking him as he looked between her and the comp boards. He hadn't considered this aspect to downloading everything into himself, of doing it in front of her.

He looked down at his hands, slowly turning them over. Synthetic skin, close to the same color as his own, covered the ports Jacoby built, removed, and rebuilt into his wrists. He hadn't used them since the day he came out of that surgery and Jacoby ordered him to download the program that would effectively cut off his voice.

Steeling himself, he pushed away the cover on his right wrist and pressed his arm into the comp board's external port.

Numbers and code flew past his vision, and he could feel it rushing into his body. It took a few seconds for him to gain his bearings, to make sense of what he was seeing and feeling and grab on to specific programs. He'd become part of the *Gray Ghost* in that moment, a breathing, living part of the ship.

He inhaled deeply, centering himself, and found the ship's master programs. He downloaded them into his enhanced brain; every blueprint and instruction manual the *Ghost* was manufactured with. Every illegal modification, details of every program. Specs of the engines and subspace engine.

And details of the subspace engine's use, namely that it hadn't been until Cecily forced it through the Highland Gate and therefore the ship had *never* been dropped out of subspace by any of her captains, ever.

He knew now what she'd been hiding.

She's never done this before. Not just dropping out, but taken the ship on a subspace route.

His blood chilled, and he fought the urge to rip his wrist out of the comp ports and confront her before everything he needed was finished downloading.

She's sick. I don't need to pile more stress on her right now.

Books about piloting that Cecily and the *Ghost*'s previous captains dumped into the comp were downloaded into his head, their words running across his vision faster than he ever thought possible, but he absorbed every word. The thrill of finally learning to fly a ship as magnificent as the *Gray Ghost* paled in light of what he'd figured out about her captain.

He disconnected from the comp ports, a little dizzy from the information overload. He looked over at Cecily, who stared at him, open-mouthed. His embarrassment rose again at giving her the reminder of what he was, and he looked away.

"Holy shit," she said, her voice a croak.

"Sorry," he mumbled. "Should've done that on the bridge."

"It's okay," she said. "I just—I hope I didn't make things weird for you."

"It isn't," he lied.

"It is," she insisted. "I'm sorry. It doesn't bother me, if that's what you were worried about."

It was, and he was worried about what she'd been hiding from him. But until the time came to drop out of subspace early or they reached its proper exit—whichever came first—there wasn't much point to fretting about her lack of experience with their situation.

But besides that, her acceptance meant a lot to him.

"Don't worry about it," he said. "I'm actually kind of tired after that overload. I could go for a nap."

"Stay here," she said. "Take your nap with me."

He froze, considering her offer.

"I'm cold," she said. "You seem like you'd be warm. And I'm not contagious. The sickbay comp said so."

Jason wasn't worried about Cecily being contagious. His programming would prevent infection, anyway. The kind of fever she had probably wasn't from a virus. He swallowed at the internal reminder.

"Okay," he said. He sat down on the bed. "Scoot over."

CHAPTER 7

CECILY'S BLEARY EYES OPENED, and it took a few seconds for her to orient herself. Her head pounded in time to her heartbeat and her tongue felt thick and furry.

And she was still so *cold*. She wrapped the blankets tighter around herself and looked on her other side for Jason, who she distinctly remembered asking to take a nap with her. She should probably be embarrassed about that, but she couldn't bring herself to be.

Another memory popped up: once again, thinking Jason was interested in her and her response to his statement that he'd never done a certain thing before.

And he meant downloading a ship's data into his head. God, I'm still a fucking idiot.

She shivered. *Make that a fucking sick idiot.*

The gravity of her situation hit her full force: she could be dying right now. She squeezed her eyes shut against the tears that threatened there.

Where did Jason go? Why did he leave me?

Just as quickly, she answered her own question. *Because he needed only a quick nap, and you're sick as a dog.*

She forced herself to sit up, muscles screaming in protest and head swimming, and tried to think about what to do next.

If she died before they could get out of subspace, Jason would be on his own. He'd have to navigate a system he was mostly unfamiliar with; probably deal with the kinds of people he didn't have any experience with. Cyborg status or not, there was a high probability that he would get himself killed without her. She had to live long enough to make sure the kill switch in his head was deactivated, and find Rordan Alexander, too.

She cursed herself for letting Alexander just take off, just like she'd cursed herself when Adam Johnston caught up with her shortly after she left him on Gamma-10. He'd had his girlfriend and a kid with him, a little girl he hadn't known existed until the day he landed there, and the sight of her just about killed Cecily. That poor kid, stuck on that hellhole of a planet.

She'd left two of the surviving cyborgs in areas transformed by war, one with a family he hadn't known about, with little thought of how they'd resettle. It hadn't even crossed her mind to direct them to help or suggest alternative destinations. Her only thought was finally tracking down Anders, making sure he was okay, and after all that, he couldn't tolerate the sight of her.

She and Jason were both rejected by their families, but in Jason's case, he hadn't deserved it.

She got out of bed on unsteady legs and found her thincomp, then brought it back to bed. She hesitated for a moment, then began a letter to be posted to her brother's transmit address as soon as they returned to realspace.

Dear Anders,

There's a pretty good chance I'm not going to see you again, so if I don't, let me explain a few things.

Jason slowly paced the *Gray Ghost*'s bridge, looking at his surroundings with a new eye. He'd stopped noticing the ridiculous velvet-covered everything and took in the technological details: the gleaming newness of the comp boards, the meticulous care taken by Cecily and the other captains the *Ghost* had.

But simmering under his newfound appreciation was apprehension and outright fear over their inevitable dropping out of subspace. And dropping out they would have to do: it wasn't just the kill switch in Jason's head, or the threat posed to Rordan Alexander, wherever he was. Cecily's cybernetic heart was sending her a clear message. It needed replacing, and soon.

He dearly hoped her fever was nothing more than a horrible coincidence, but if it wasn't... he didn't want to consider that.

The galaxy would be a darker place without Cecily Barris in it. During their short time aboard the *Ghost* together, he'd come to greatly care for her.

And Anders did, too. But like Jason, he was recovering from trauma. That affected familial relationships.

Cecily was recovering from trauma, too.

She clammed up every time the subject of her life after Anders was spirited away came up. Jason knew the barest details, as did Anders and Valenna, but she'd never really talked about what happened. Wasn't that a hallmark of trauma?

Maybe she'd want to open up to him after she recovered. And she *would* recover, Jason decided. He could download every byte of the sickbay's knowledge into his head if he wanted.

He needed her to be all right, to get another chance at life.

His internal chronometer told him it was nearly dinner, and he went to the galley-lounge to fix a quick meal and generate something for Cecily. Once there, he decided on soup and sandwiches and carried them to her cabin.

He knocked on the door, and when there wasn't a forthcoming invitation, gently eased it open. Cecily was sleeping still in bed where he'd left her, a thincomp on the covers.

Against his better judgement, he leaned over to read the words on the screen:

Dear Anders,

There's a pretty good chance I'm not going to see you again, so if I don't, let me explain a few things.

First, I get it. I'm not mad at you anymore for being pissed off over the whole mercenary, killer-for-hire thing. You're not cool with it, and I get that. But please understand that I did what I had to in order to survive in a war zone, and even get ahead a little financially.

Jason knew that Cecily's financial gain was more than just a little, and Anders likely did, too.

No one wants to be a mercenary for hire when they're a kid, unless they're pretty fucked up. Remember the little sociopath who lived across the street from us growing up? I think his name was Saul? I bet he would have loved to be a mercenary or bounty hunter, but he was so dumb he would have accidentally blown himself up.

I just want you to know that I love you so much, and if my heart fails while I'm stuck in subspace, know that I really wanted to do right by you.

I know you wanted to do the same thing. If I say that I appreciate what you did, it'll probably come across as condescending or something because you tell people you appreciate what they did after they buy you a coffee when you're having a shitty day at work. So, I'll say that I was shocked that you agreed to be a cyborg (and I know you didn't consent to the degree that crazy fucker Jacoby altered you). I was horrified that you'd do that to yourself, for me. But touched, too.

It made me cry, you bastard.

You didn't have to do that, but you did. And there aren't enough ways I can think of to adequately tell you how much your sacrifice meant.

Even if I end up dying, please know that it wasn't in vain.

I hope it wasn't.

I love you.

Cecily

P.S. Hang on to Valenna. She's a treasure.

Jason looked away, guilt suffusing him. *I shouldn't have read that.*

Cecily stirred, vision fixing on him. She turned the thincomp over so he couldn't see the screen, then looked at the tray. "What's that?"

"Dinner."

"What time is it?"

"About half-past five."

She rubbed her eyes and sat up. "I'm not that hungry."

"The sickbay comp said you need to stay hydrated. Do you want to get up or have dinner in bed?"

"Bed's fine." She sat up and accepted a mug of clear soup.

Jason unclipped a chair from its deck lock near the cabin's viewport and set it down next to her bed, then picked up his sandwich. Neither of them spoke while they ate.

Cecily was the one to break the silence. "You read my letter to Anders."

He dropped his sandwich, the motion drawing a small smile to her face.

"I don't know if I'm going to send it to him," she said. "I was going to tell him about my heart transplant and all that, but I just don't want to think about that time in my life. It sucked."

That had to be one of the biggest understatements Jason ever heard.

"For a cyborg soldier, you're not that stealthy. I heard you come in."

"Maybe you're a light sleeper."

"Yeah, it helps to be in this line of work."

"I'm sorry," he said. "I shouldn't have read it."

She shrugged. "I'm not mad. Anders might have shown it to you anyway."

"No," Jason replied. "He wouldn't have."

"Oh?" She eyed him over her mug's rim.

"You aren't going to send him that goodbye letter, because you're not going to die."

Another tiny smile tugged at the corners of her mouth. "Have you developed a new cybernetic heart? Or come across a compatible humanoid heart I forgot about in cold storage?"

The memory of the cold storage containers in the hold—specifically, the memory of his fallen cyborg brothers-in-arms in them—rose in Jason's mind. He hadn't been in the *Gray Ghost*'s hold since he was rescued, and if he had his way, he'd never step foot there again. "It's fucked up that you can joke about having organs in your hold when you probably have at some point."

"I ran some organs for the right price, so yeah."

"Good God and stars above."

"You didn't answer my question. Did you come across a new heart somewhere?"

"No," Jason said. "I just—I need you to stay alive. So does Anders."

"I don't want to die, you know. I'm really hoping this stupid fever is just a fluke." But there was uncertainty in her voice, and Jason's sensors told him her temperature was still running way too high.

"So do I."

"You can fly the ship now," she pointed out. "You'd be okay after the *Ghost* exits in realspace."

"I wish you'd stop talking like you've resigned yourself to dying," Jason said. His appetite gone, he set aside the remains of his sandwich.

"It's a hazard in my profession. Frankly, I'm surprised I've made it this long, cybernetic heart or not."

"I also wish you'd stop being so flip."

She narrowed her eyes at him. "I'll be fucking flip if I feel like it, Jason. I've earned it."

That sounded a little more like the Cecily he knew and cared about, and he relaxed a little. "All right."

"All right, you agree with me?"

"All right, I'm not arguing with you."

She set her soup mug on the nightstand and lay back against the pillow. "I need more sleep. Stay with me again?"

If only to make sure she wasn't getting worse, Jason was happy to oblige. He nodded and slipped into bed next to her.

Cecily knew sleeping next to someone would be comforting, but she hadn't realized how much.

Not just someone. Even though her muscles protested as she did so, she rolled over just enough to steal a glance at Jason. He was sleeping, or at least faking it, and she closed her eyes again, not wanting to disturb him.

He was so *warm*.

Cyborgs probably have internal heaters or something.

She smiled in the darkness, but it quickly faded as she realized why she craved his body heat.

It was Jason himself, dependable and unflappable. Who'd uploaded manuals and schematics and blueprints into his head, to be a better partner to her. To be her equal. He respected her experience and didn't even seem that bothered by her career, considering his own background.

But another darker, more ominous reason lurked behind her warm feelings for Jason.

She could feel her fever getting worse, her body growing sicker. She knew, deep down, that her fever wasn't a fluke. Her cybernetic heart was failing, and she had no idea how much longer she had. She couldn't guess if she had a chance at recovering just enough to drop out the *Gray Ghost* back to realspace and set a course to save Jason's life.

He hadn't signed up to administer palliative care to her or shove his head so full of information that the impact left him unsteady and weak.

But as she drifted off to sleep again, she couldn't think of a solution that was certain to save both of them.

CHAPTER 8

JASON WOKE up a few hours later, fully rested even though it was past two in the morning. Cecily slept on, her back to him, but her vitals had changed enough to alarm him.

His ocular enhancements noted that her fever still hadn't broken, which was concerning enough. But he could see that her breathing was shallow, more erratic, and her sleep was somehow ... deeper, he guessed. None of that made sense.

He gently shook her shoulder. "Cecily."

She slept on.

"*Cecily*." His voice grew more urgent, his grip a little tighter. "Wake up."

Now that he was touching her, more information about her state flowed to him, and his stomach turned over in fear.

She was in a coma.

It was a symptom of heart failure; his mass information download told him as much. His mind raced, trying to figure out what to do next.

"Hey," he said aloud. "Uh, ship? *Gray Ghost*?"

The cabin lights flickered.

"What's the procedure for a coma patient?" he asked.

"Please proceed to the sickbay," the comp's voice said.

"Can I help her there?"

"Further information is available in the sickbay," came the reply.

"Why can't you tell me here?"

"For purposes of storage optimization in the computer banks, all medical-related information is located there."

"Okay. Can you tell me if there's anything about hearts there? Uh, cardiology?"

"Information is available about human systems in the sickbay."

Jason gritted his teeth and got out of bed. "Thanks."

He carefully collected Cecily in his arms, for the second time in as many days, and carried her to the sickbay. If he didn't know any better, if his nanobots hadn't automatically relayed the relevant data to him about her condition, he would've sworn she was smaller than she was last time he held her.

She hadn't stirred by the time he lay her on the sickbay's diag bed and activated its cover. "Sickbay comp," he said, voice bouncing off the walls. He hoped he'd addressed the system in a way it would understand.

"Yes?" said a disembodied voice, similar to the one in Cecily's cabin. "How may I be of assistance?"

"I think the captain's cybernetic heart is failing," Jason said. "I think she's in a coma."

"The sickbay system cannot perform surgery."

"Of course not, but can you diagnose her?"

"The diag bed is online and available for such a purpose."

Jason felt like punching something. "Stars take it," he muttered, an oath from Renza.

"Please repeat your command."

Now he understood why Cecily relied on written information in the sickbay. "If I run these tests on the diag bed," he said, "can you help me make sense of them? Do you have any information at all on cybernetic hearts or the captain's medical files?"

"Medical definitions can be provided. The captain's medical files are stored here."

"All right, now we're getting somewhere."

"Please repeat your command."

"Disregard that command. Can I see Cecily's medical files?"

"That information is prohibited without Captain Barris's authorization."

God damn it. Jason fought to keep his voice level and instead looked at the diag bed's report, projected on the same holo display where he'd looked at his superimposed cybernetic body.

The data there was grim. As he'd suspected, she was in a coma, and she needed another heart transplant.

He looked down at his hands, how they shook from nerves. This was well beyond his knowledge; even if he could download everything related to cybernetic cardiology into himself, he'd be too terrified about nicking something vital to perform emergency surgery.

There was some other data there, too: model and serial numbers for her heart. "Sickbay," he said. "What can you tell me about the cybernetic heart in Cecily? It's a Gara-Holt heart, model D eighty-six." He rattled off its serial number.

"Gara-Holt cybernetic hearts have been discontinued," the voice said.

Jason froze. Had Cecily known that? "Explain," he demanded.

"These hearts were officially discontinued for liability purposes when Gara-Holt Medical Holdings was dissolved and absorbed into Zone Medical Futures."

"When did this happen?"

"Thirteen weeks ago."

"What were the liability reasons?"

"The Gara-Holt hearts have a design flaw, and Zone Medical Futures urged their recipients to have them replaced."

It was no fucking wonder that Cecily didn't speak to the sickbay computer. It had its own design flaw in that it wouldn't get to the fucking point. "Can you elaborate on its design flaw?" Jason asked, keeping his temper in check.

"The hearts could stop functioning or function intermittently based on the recipient's physical responses to external stimuli or the environment. Notably, recipients experienced cardiac distress during extended time aboard starfaring ships."

"Why would that happen?"

"Gara-Holt did not elaborate."

"Of course, they didn't. Why wasn't this released publicly?"

"The acquisition was announced in the Zone media."

And Cecily didn't spend much time in the Zone these days, and even if she did, the news was largely dominated by politicians talking about the war's end. Then there was the issue that corporations could largely do whatever they wanted in the Zone, with few legal repercussions. Any announcements about the faulty hears probably would have been made in the middle of the night, on the most obscure news broadcasts, if Jason's experience was anything to go by.

"Is there anything here that I can use or anything I can do to extend the life of Cecily's heart?" he asked.

"Gara-Holt recommended that affected hearts be restarted until they can be replaced."

Jason glanced at Cecily, so still and pale under the diag bed cover. Her breathing was more labored now. "Can that be done to Cecily?" he asked. "And what are the risks?"

"Defective units may not start beating again."

Without taking his eyes off her, he asked, "Can you

determine Cecily's chances of recovery if her heart is restarted?"

"Gara-Holt's guidelines indicated that the chance was fifty percent."

Jason closed his eyes, trying to form a plan. "What's Cecily's status now?"

"Captain Barris's cybernetic heart is failing, and she is in a coma."

"How long does she have to live?" His voice cracked.

"In this current state, between four and nineteen hours."

"Fuck." A lump formed in his throat and he felt tears pricking at his eyes for the first time in years.

His cybernetics took care of all that and instead began to calculate Cecily's risks based on the information he'd been given. He didn't need to rely on his machinery to know he was faced with a hideous choice.

She had a fifty-fifty chance of surviving her heart being restarted.

She had a one hundred percent chance of dying before they left subspace if it wasn't.

"Okay," he said, voice unsteady. "How do I restart her heart?"

"The diag bed will restart her heart."

"Stars save me," he muttered.

"Please repeat your command."

"Nothing," he said. "How is her heart restarted? Can it even be done in here?"

"The diag bed is equipped to restart a cybernetic heart."

"She won't have to be cut open?"

"The equipment in this sickbay is not designed for major surgery. It can perform this procedure using electric pulses transmitted through the body."

It made sense. "Why is it so risky then?"

"The risk is due to a design flaw in the cybernetic heart

model. This procedure is considered very high risk as the patient's heart will have to be shut down and restarted. The patient's heartbeat will not resume for at least thirty seconds. At most, the patient's heartbeat will not resume for four minutes."

She would be technically dead after four minutes of cardiac inactivity, wouldn't she? "When is the procedure considered a failure?" he asked.

"When the patient's heat does not resume normal activity after four minutes."

He didn't have a choice. This was the only shot Cecily had at living long enough to get out of subspace and find a qualified surgeon to replace her heart. At this point, Jason no longer cared about his kill switch. All that mattered was her recovery.

"Okay," he said. "Let's do it."

"Please state your command clearly."

"Sickbay, restart Cecily's cybernetic heart," he said, carefully enunciating each word.

The diag bed cover whirred and a few lights blinked. A whine filled the air, and Cecily's vitals dramatically changed, both on the holo display and Jason's ocular enhancements.

No heartbeat detected.

A tear escaped his eye, and he wiped it away impatiently.

Had he just killed her?

Cecily didn't move, and she stopped breathing.

A few seconds later, the diag bed crackled with energy. In the sickbay's small space, it was as loud as a peal of thunder on Jason's home planet.

Another crackle of energy, then another. "What's happening?" he asked, his panic rising.

"The restart procedure has begun," the voice said, too sunnily for Jason's liking.

The diag bed sent more energy pulses into Cecily, and her head lolled to the side. Her nostrils flared.

"Heartbeat detected," the sickbay comp announced. "Initiating final procedure sequence."

One more jolt of power later and Cecily's arms and legs jerked.

"Normal heartbeat function has resumed," the comp said. "It is advised that the patient seek heart replacement at an accredited hospital as soon as possible."

Jason rushed to the diag bed and grasped Cecily's hand. She turned her head in his direction and coughed. "Cecily," he said urgently. "Wake up."

Her eyes fluttered open. "What's going on?" She tried to sit up but was blocked by the diag bed cover.

Jason deactivated it, and it slid away. "Thank God and the stars," he said and wrapped her in a hug.

Her arms immediately slipped around his neck. "You didn't answer my question."

"You went into a coma," he said into her hair. "You would've died if I hadn't done it."

"Still not answering."

"I told the comp to restart your heart," he said. "Did you know yours was discontinued?"

"What the hell?" She sounded shocked. "No. I just knew it was failing."

"It has a design flaw and the company that made it folded recently. I guess you didn't know, but the *Ghost* would've picked up all the news bulletins from comm beacons, which is why the comp knew, but..." He pulled away enough to look at her, still confused. "You're okay for now. You were dead for a minute."

Her eyes were huge, a little glassy. "You restarted my heart?"

He nodded. "You were only a few hours away from

dying."

"Oh, my God."

He didn't know who moved first, but before he knew it, his lips were pressed against hers in a passionate kiss that sucked the breath from him. All too quickly, it was over, and he broke their contact.

"Cecily," he said. "Sorry. I..."

But she surprised him when she kissed him again, arms tightening around him, bringing him closer to her. Her tongue teased his lips apart and he leaned into her, needing more, and all thoughts of what had just happened flew from his mind.

All that mattered and would ever matter was that Cecily was still alive.

By the time he broke the kiss, both of them were breathing hard, and he pressed his forehead against hers, savoring the contact. Every nerve in his body commanded him to kiss her again, take her back to her cabin and show her how much he'd come to care for her, but he didn't.

"Don't ever apologize," Cecily said.

Unsure how to answer, he merely nodded.

"If I'm okay for now, I think I'll go back to bed," she said. Then, almost as an afterthought, she added, "To sleep."

She hopped off the diag bed, taking a few seconds to steady herself, and before she left the sickbay, squeezed his hand. "Thank you," she said.

"You'd do the same for me."

She tilted her head to the side, expression inscrutable except for her dilated pupils, something his sensors picked up immediately. "I would, you know? I like you. Probably more than I should."

Before she left the sickbay, she said over her shoulder, "That's more a statement about the kind of person I am, rather than you are, by the way."

CHAPTER 9

CECILY SLEPT UNTIL NEARLY NOON, waking up refreshed and alert. And *alive*, she noted wryly as she combed her hair, damp from a shower, and dressed.

She needed to read and watch the news broadcasts more often. Knowing that her cybernetic heart wasn't just failing, but that the model itself was discontinued and its manufacturer absorbed into another corporation... she shivered at how close she came to death. Had Jason not thought to ask the sickbay comp what to do—she rarely did, since the stupid thing tended to meander, wasting energy— she would probably have died in her sleep already.

Another, different kind of shiver danced down her spine when she thought of Jason.

He kissed me!

She caught sight of her goofy smile in the mirror. She was blushing like a schoolgirl.

When was the last time I was so happy about a kiss?

She couldn't remember, although she'd had a boyfriend before Anders disappeared and she had her heart transplant. But she'd never felt so giddy over a man in her twenty-four years.

"Where's Jason?" she asked the cabin comp.

"Jason is in the sim chamber," came the automatic response.

Leaving her damp hair loose, she left her cabin and made her way to the lounge for a late breakfast of tea and a pastry. While she ate, she considered how to approach Jason when she saw him next.

She hoped things wouldn't get weird between them. At least, not the bad kind of weird.

When she'd finished eating and left the dishes in the recycler, she crossed the corridor to the sim chamber and steeled herself. Butterflies ran riot in her stomach.

She pressed the door key and it slid open with a whisper. She stepped into a simulation similar to the campfire one from a few nights ago. The fire was lower and the sun was rising in a blend of deep oranges and reds that made Cecily almost wish she still lived planetside.

And Jason sat facing away from her, watching the artificial sun rise.

She joined him and wished she'd thought to bring him coffee or something to eat. "Hi," she said.

"Good morning. How are you feeling?"

"Better than I have in days." She stretched her legs out and crossed them at the ankle. "Thank you for what you did last night." She corrected herself. "This morning. You know what I mean."

"Yeah. And no thanks necessary. You would've done the same for me."

Cecily thought about what he said for a moment, how she would've reacted had it been him laid up with a malfunctioning kill switch in his head and she had to take care of him. She wasn't sure she would've known what to do. There was less information aboard about his physiology than hers.

That realization made her understand something else.

"We have to drop out of subspace," she said. "As soon as possible." Any heady, romantic feelings she was harboring were replaced by stark fear of the unknown.

"Well, that escalated quickly," Jason said.

She shook her head, as if doing so would organize the thoughts tumbling around there. "I mean, the best way for me to help you is to get us out of here," she said. "I don't have equivalent information here about you. If the worst happens, I don't know if I can restart you."

She hated using the word "restart" in relation to his head, like he was a robot. Just so he didn't believe she operated on those lines, she quickly added, "I meant..."

"I know what you meant. And I know that you don't know if you can drop out the *Gray Ghost* from subspace and keep us alive."

If she hadn't been sitting, she would have collapsed at those words. As it was, her heart beat so quickly that for a second she thought it was failing again. But it resumed its normal pace, and she said, "Oh?"

"I downloaded a lot of data when I connected to the port in your cabin. I have the *Ghost*'s entire history in me, including everything about her subspace engine and her need for servicing at some point soon, and how she's never been dropped out." He faced her, dark eyes meeting hers. This close, she could see their metallic glint more clearly. Could his sensors pick up that she'd been lying to him by omission, that she'd never pulled a ship out of subspace without an exit gate?

"She's never been dropped out. I already told you that." she said, voice breathy. Their conversation was serious, but he still had an effect on her that was almost hypnotic.

"Have you ever dropped out *any* ship from subspace?"

She could tell from his tone that he already knew the answer. She may as well be honest with him. "No."

"Do you think you can do it?"

She wanted to lie to him, to hear herself tell him yes. Because if he believed her, then she might be able to conjure up enough confidence in herself to get at the bridge's controls and force the ship out of subspace.

It would be the most dangerous thing she'd ever done. She included the last years performing murders-for-hire for dangerous people and crashing Garrett Jacoby's cyborg facilities on Omega-Three-Omega. Between her heart being restarted and the impending drop out, she'd never been more aware of her mortality, including before her transplant. And she'd been fairly certain then that she was going to die.

He was waiting for an answer. He deserved a truthful one.

"I don't know," she finally said.

He was quiet, and she waited for him to say something, *anything*. Although the last thing she wanted to hear from him was false encouragement. Cecily had never appreciated being told that all she had to do was believe in herself to make something happen, like that was a substitute for education and experience.

After what felt like an eternity, Jason asked, "Do you think the *Gray Ghost* is capable of dropping out?"

That was something she could confidently answer. "Yes," she said. "The technology's there, even if it isn't the greatest." Her voice became a little stronger, and she felt a little surer of what was ahead, what she'd have to do. "I'm not worried about pushing the ship beyond her capabilities. I'm worried about doing something wrong and killing us both."

And, by extension, killing Marshall Caron and Rordan Alexander, wherever he was. Or possibly her brother, should someone come sniffing around for the tech in his body.

"What do you need me to do?" he asked.

She considered the question for a few seconds. Lascivious thoughts popped into her head, which wasn't helpful, and she closed her eyes, concentrating. "You have the gist of piloting," she said. "You know the ship inside and out by now, right?"

"I don't have any practical flight experience. You know that."

"But if you were plunked down at the controls in the copilot's seat, you could monitor the ship," she said. "Keep an eye on life support, engine function, all that?"

"Probably."

"That's what I'd need you to do," she said. "I can take the ship out of subspace while you make sure she isn't about to explode."

"I can do that," he said. "I'd be happy to. I don't like feeling useless."

"I don't want you to feel like you *have* to do this," Cecily replied. "You weren't obligated to help."

"You don't want me to feel like I'm back on Oh-Three-Oh," Jason deduced.

She nodded. "Yeah."

The sun rose a little higher, but the sim chamber's sensors dimmed it enough to keep from blinding them. Not that it would matter much to someone with ocular enhancements.

"Is this from Renza?" she asked.

"It isn't precise, but it's close. Renza has two suns." He leaned back and stretched out his legs. "You'd think for a planet with two suns it would be a little warmer, but you'd be wrong."

"The sun hardly came out when I was growing up," Cecily said, surprising herself.

"Oh?"

"Anders and I are from Danton," she said. "Do you know it?"

"It's close to Echo-7, isn't it?"

"Yeah. We escaped as soon as our parents died. We moved around space stations and other, cheaper planets until Anders enlisted. He sent me money for hospital visits and stays in boarding cubes until his tour was over." She still remembered the message he'd sent her when he agreed to cyborg enhancement. It was the last she'd heard of him until she found him on Omega-Three-Omega four years later.

"What made you into a mercenary?"

Cecily had known the subject would come up at some point, and in a weird sort of way, was almost looking forward to it. It would be a relief to get her history off her chest, tell it to a man who she suspected wouldn't judge her too harshly for it.

At least, she hoped he wouldn't. She liked and respected him too much, and his opinion of her was important.

He picked up her hesitation and quickly added, "If you're not uncomfortable talking about it."

She shrugged. It was a simpler story that he was probably expecting. "My new heart did wonders," she said. "I was back up and doing normal things just a couple of days after I had the transplant. It was arranged by a black market contractor I found on the worst parts of the galactic net, and I had to do some favors for him after." She barked out a short, humorless laugh. "He meant killing people via poison. It turns out I really liked being and feeling alive, and a heart that worked made me feel invincible."

"Mercenary work is dangerous," Jason said. "You didn't consider that it could shorten your life expectancy?"

He had a point, one she'd considered before. "Not really," she said. "It was a way to make enough money to retire on and gave me the contacts to find out what happened to Anders. The military said he'd gone AWOL when I asked, but I knew that wasn't true."

"Anders isn't one to abandon his responsibilities."

"I know." The thought of her brother, one of the most honorable men she'd ever known, brought a lump to her throat. She missed him and their previous, close relationship, fiercely.

She didn't want to think about that right now. She knew she wasn't invincible and her current healthy state was temporary.

She steered the subject back to prematurely exiting subspace. "I told you before that I think we should drop out as soon as possible and we should make plans for it."

"Do you have a time in mind?"

She thought quickly. "Probably tonight," she said. "Or the middle of the night. If the Scout is out there, we'll have a better chance of taking them by surprise at that time." If the Scout pilot knew anything about subspace gates and routes in the Brava System, and Cecily would be surprised if he didn't, the pilot could calculate roughly where the *Gray Ghost* could be in relation to realspace. There were other subspace gates near the Highland one; the Scout was likely in one of those routes now.

"Do Scout pilots work nine to five or something?"

Frustration edged into her voice. "Not that I know of, but *I* prefer to work at night. It's been in my experience that people aren't expecting a visit then. We'll have an advantage."

"Okay." But there was still doubt in his voice.

She didn't feel like taking that on right now, either. Her original intention of coming in here—thanking him for saving her life, asking him what he thought about their kiss last night, seeing how he felt—fell by the wayside, and without another word, she stood up and left the sim chamber.

Jason knew he was being difficult and rude about the impending drop out when he spoke with Cecily, and it was hard to pinpoint exactly why. Fear? He'd already faced death and, while confined to Omega-Three-Omega, thought his fate there was worse than it.

She wanted to talk to him. She was trying to open up, get his opinion on something that would deeply affect both of them, and he'd brushed her off while staring at a weak simulation of the Renza sunrise.

Stars fucking damn it.

He usually wasn't the kind of person who'd turn into a galaxy-class jerkoff after he kissed someone, although it was so long since that last happened that things might have changed without his knowing. He'd have to work on that.

The sun rose a little higher, glowing brighter. It was a pretty sight, but it didn't stir up any homesickness in him for Renza or even Kurkay-2. He missed shooting the shit with Anders and Valenna, but that was all.

He shut off the simulation, the brilliant sunrise quickly replaced by thermowire-striped walls, and left the sim chamber in search of Cecily.

But she wasn't in sickbay, the bridge, the lounge, or her cabin. Those were the only places he could think of where she'd be, the only places she'd shown him.

The engine room.

He'd needled her about the subspace engine, hadn't he? If nothing else, a trip to the engine room would give him the chance to look at the machinery he'd already learned so much about.

He took the stairs down to the *Gray Ghost*'s lowest deck, the one with the cargo hold where he and the other cyborgs, living and dead, had been transported away from Oh-Three-Oh. His mind flashed back to Aaron Bell's body hitting the floor and looked away.

His brothers-in-arms who hadn't made it off the base alive had to be cremated, their remains interred in a nondescript private civilian cemetery close to Anders and Valenna's farm. Their remains were buried under false names, all in an attempt to throw off anyone looking to reverse engineer what remained of them.

He paused, closed his eyes, and swallowed the lump that had formed in his throat before heading for the engine room at the end of the corridor.

The engines' hum grew louder as he approached, and when he tried the door, he found it wasn't locked. He paused in the doorway, taking in the sight.

The room was much larger than he expected, for one thing. The standard engine dominated the room and mostly matched the images he'd downloaded of it, except its energy core was pulsing a brighter green than he thought it would. He supposed that was a good thing. An energy core glowing red meant they were about to die.

The room's walls were lined with comp boards of varying sizes, some obviously installed long after the *Gray Ghost* made her maiden voyage. Some had been deactivated altogether, their screens dark and wires protruding from them after they'd been salvaged for components. Jason slowly walked around the room, looking for the subspace engine that had to be here somewhere.

He found it, a few meters away from the standard engine, smaller than he thought it would be, standing at just under two meters. Its energy core lazily alternated between green and yellow pulses, both of which were acceptable according to the specs Jason downloaded.

And crouched in front of it, a control panel wrenched open, was Cecily. A tool case rested on the deck beside her, and she held a laser splicer in her hand. A protective headset covered her ears. She looked up when she saw Jason, and he had the distinct impression that she was trying to keep herself from rolling her eyes at the sight of him.

"Hi," he said, his voice nearly drowned out by the engines' din.

She replaced the laser splicer in her tool case and stood up, then pointed in the doorway's direction. He followed her to the corridor, and she took off the headphones.

Cecily crossed her arms and waited for him to speak.

"I owe you an apology," he said.

She raised an eyebrow. "Oh?"

"You came by to say thank you, and you were nice to me, and I just brushed you off," he said. "I'm sorry about that."

She was quiet for a few seconds, thinking. "You're hard to read, do you know that?"

"I don't mean to be."

"Well, shit, no one means to be. And I know I'm hard to read sometimes, too, but I'm working on that. I've tried to be upfront with you about all of this."

"You didn't tell me you've never dropped out of subspace before."

"God damn it." She looked away. "Can we just agree that we both fucked up?"

He nodded. "That works."

She looked back at the engine room. "Everything's fine in there. The subspace engine's a little old but still works just fine. There isn't any technical reason why dropping out shouldn't work." She took a deep breath and slowly exhaled. "It's all on the pilot."

"And you'll be able to do it."

A nervous laugh escaped her. "I appreciate your faith in me."

"You've fought to survive in worse conditions than this," Jason said. "And now you have help."

Surprise widened her eyes. "I guess I do."

He tapped his head. "And that help has everything about this ship—every spec, every blueprint—in his head, ready to tell you whatever you need to know, when you need to know it."

She nodded, and he could tell his words had their desired effect. She was feeling a little better about what lay ahead. "Yeah."

There was something else he needed to tell her, and it was better to do it now, while they were still alive. "Cecily."

She tilted her head to the side, waiting for him to continue.

A wave of shyness washed over him, and he was unsure how to form his next words. "About last night."

A blush stained her cheeks, and some of his nervousness dissipated.

"Restarting your heart scared the shit out of me," he said. "I don't think anything, ever, will make me feel like that again. But I'm glad I did it." He didn't try to hide the longing in his voice, wanting her to hear it. "The universe needs you."

That drew another small laugh from her.

He hesitated for a second before he said, "I need you, too."

She launched herself at him, but his cybernetics had him reacting before his brain registered what was happening. He welcomed her kiss, arms locking around her, tongue sweeping into her mouth. White-hot desire thrummed through his body, igniting feelings that he thought he'd lost when he became a cyborg, and all worries of what lay ahead for them vanished.

She broke their kiss, her breath coming hard. He knew his was, too. "Do you want to go to my cabin?" she asked, and he heard a note of doubt in her voice, one that shouldn't be there.

"Why not mine?"

"The captain's cabin is closer."

He scooped her up in his arms in one smooth motion,

eliciting a gasp from her, so different from his carrying her to the sickbay the night before. "Let's go."

Anticipation coiled low in Cecily's belly, and she clung to Jason like a lifeline.

I need you, too.

She rolled his words over in her mind, warmth spreading through her when she thought of them. She knew the meaning behind them wasn't purely physical; they could be on the brink of starting something she'd never let herself dream about.

Mercenaries with faulty hearts weren't allowed the luxury of relationships or love.

Without missing a beat, he slid open her cabin door and made a beeline for her bed, still unmade, but he didn't appear to care. He set her down with a grace she wouldn't have expected from a cyborg, then surprised her when he lay down next to her, propped up on his side.

She did the same. "Is anything wrong?"

"No," he said. "Not at all." Embarrassment shadowed his features. "I just haven't done this in a really long time."

"I'm not surprised to hear that," she said gently. "And I don't care."

"Just—so you know."

She shrugged as best she could from her position. "That doesn't change anything for me."

His reply was another kiss, with more gentleness than she expected, but it still sent a bolt of heat through her. He eased her on her back without breaking that contact, one of his hands finding her shirt's hem and sliding beneath it to trace patterns on her skin.

His fingertips were a little rough, the ports in them delivering just enough friction to set all her nerve endings alight. She moved against his hand in encouragement, and he obliged, pulling away from her just enough so he could help her peel off her shirt.

Her skin broke out in goosebumps as he took in the sight of her, pupils dilating in a way that she knew had nothing to do with his cybernetics. "Your turn," she said and reached for his black T-shirt.

Jason hesitated for half a second, then pulled it over his head.

Cecily sucked in a breath of appreciation. She'd expected him to be in shape: she'd felt it when he held her, saw the outlines of well-honed muscles through his clothing. Seeing him in the flesh was another thing.

And his skin was heavily crisscrossed with thick, ropy scars, scored with places where ports and components had been inserted and removed. She didn't care about them but knew he did. The relatively small scar between her breasts where she'd had her heart transplanted paled in comparison.

And the last thing she wanted right now was for him to feel self-conscious or insecure.

She reached for the seal on his pants, and she thought she could see him relax a little.

But he didn't move to take them off once she'd opened them, and instead covered her body with his own, mouths fusing, hands roving over her body. His lips kissed a trail down her neck, finding the sensitive spot under her ear and lightly biting it, marking her.

The motion was small, but it set off something primal in her, and she needed to feel him skin-to-skin, needed to get rid of the clothes separating them.

Her sharp gasp seemed to spur him into action, and his hands pulled at her bra, at her pants, and faster than she expected, the rest of their clothes were gone, tossed somewhere on the cabin's deck.

His erection bobbed against her thigh, teasing her, and her knees slid apart of their own volition inviting him closer. Jason's body fitted itself against hers, settling between her legs, and without missing a beat, pushed inside her.

A sharp cry escaped her just as Jason groaned, and he pressed his forehead against hers, not moving. Cecily wiggled a little around him to adjust, drawing another groan from him.

"Are you okay?" he finally managed to ask.

She hooked one leg around him, drawing him closer. "Very."

That was all the encouragement he needed. His body surged against hers, and she gladly welcomed him, already feeling the thrum of a climax building in her.

She bit his shoulder when it hit her, and that seemed to spur him on. He moved faster inside her, and the irregular pant of his breath in her ear told her he was close, too. He stiffened against her, her name on his lips before he captured her mouth with his and laced his fingers through hers, cybernetic hearts beating in tandem.

CHAPTER 10

IT WAS past midnight when Jason and Cecily made their way to the bridge, ready to drop the *Gray Ghost* from subspace.

He was glad they'd spent the day together, exploring each other's bodies and making love. If he had to die today, he mused, that wasn't a bad way to spend his final hours.

He sneaked a glance at Cecily in the velvet-covered pilot's seat, brow furrowed in concentration as she looked at the ship's readings on the console before her. She caught him and gave him a nervous smile.

He responded by squeezing her hand. "We're going to get through this."

She nodded, but he saw the fear and doubt in her expression.

"We're going to get through this," he repeated, "and then you can start your life over anonymously in the Brava System, if you want."

"What about you?" she asked. "Are you going back to Anders and Valenna's place?"

Did he want to? He had every intention of staying Bravan space. There wasn't anything left for him in the Zone. But did he want to keep living with Anders and Valenna, or start over somewhere else in the system?

Maybe with Cecily?

You're getting ahead of yourself, Formosa.

But was he?

Cecily was still waiting for a reply. "I don't know," he said honestly, then took a deep breath and added, "Things have changed for me."

That answer seemed to mollify her. "Me, too."

She didn't elaborate, but instead returned to the command console, tapping in a course for dropping out the ship. Warnings flashed across both of their screens, the bridge's emergency lights glowed, and the disembodied comp voice said, "Premature ejection from the Highland subspace route is not recommended."

"Of course, it isn't," grumbled Cecily, then typed an override code into the console.

"Voice authorization necessary," the comp voice said.

She sighed, then said, "Cecily Barris authorizing the ejection. Please proceed with my original commands."

"Acknowledged."

The ship's engines rumbled under their feet, louder than Jason anticipated. The volume was alarming, but according to the system readout on the copilot's console and the specs he'd downloaded into himself, nothing was set to explode just yet.

An explosion would be instant death.

What if the drop out impact is so great it shut off the life support and they suffocated instead?

He pushed those thoughts away. He couldn't afford to dwell on the what-ifs right now.

The comp voice intoned, "Early ejection from subspace may result in weakness in the ship's hull integrity."

"I know," said Cecily, but her voice was mostly drowned out by the engine's noise.

"Early ejection from subspace may result in critical system failures from impact."

"I know!" Cecily snapped. "Fuck! Just fucking do it!"

Jason watched as she overrode safety protocols, and he projected a star chart on the holo display between the seats. It pinpointed where they were roughly, in relation to realspace, to minimize the possibility of dropping out too close to a random spaceport or a busy space lane. Other than dying in a hull breach or suffocation, the last thing he wanted was to be mowed down in traffic by a ship larger than the *Gray Ghost*.

But it looked like it was uninhabited space around their estimated drop out site, in a remote quadrant of the Brava System. Perfect.

The ship tilted sharply to the starboard side, and its force had Jason's safety harness's straps biting into his side. "Damn it!" yelled Cecily.

The *Gray Ghost*'s red alert klaxons activated, drowning out any other possibility of talking.

Was that supposed to happen?

Cecily pressed something on her console, and a set of manual controls popped up. She clasped its hand grips and steered like the ship was nothing more than an antigrav ground flitter and she was out for a leisurely float around a park.

The ship banked again, harder this time, nearly sideways.

"Fuck!" yelled Jason, but his voice disappeared in the alarms.

"Please examine the gravity controls at your earliest convenience," said the comp voice, sounding far too calm for Jason's liking. As if on cue, he felt like he was being pulled into the deck itself, to become one with the ship.

Cecily was sweating, fighting against the malfunctioning gravity as she hand-flew the ship.

The *Gray Ghost* nosedived, and the engines sounded even louder to Jason.

This is it. This is how I die.

White blurs populated the viewscreen, then the ship jerked forward, and the blurs formed into stars. The *Ghost* righted itself and stilled. The subspace engine went silent.

Jason hardly dared to breathe.

"Gravity controls automatically corrected," said the comp voice. "The ship has successfully ejected from Highland subspace."

"Holy shit," Cecily whispered. She unsnapped her safety harness and stood up, wonder across her face as she stared at stars projected across the viewscreen. "We did it!"

Jason did likewise and noticed as he rose that his muscles were stiff from involuntarily clenching them. But that didn't stop him from closing the short distance between them and sweeping her up in his arms for a searing kiss. "*You* did it," he corrected her.

"No," she said, a smile blooming across her face. "I couldn't have done this without you. I would've just waited until the gate exit, days away, and hoped for the best."

"You wouldn't have done that," he said. "You're the captain of the *Gray Ghost*. You're one of the most feared and reliable mercenaries in Bravan and Zone space."

Any retort she might have offered was interrupted by a new alert from the ship. "Ships detected," Cecily said, glancing at a console. "But it's my long-range, and they're still a couple of hours away at their current speeds."

"Idents?"

She gave him a look that he swore made his heart skip a beat. "I love it when you talk like a captain." She swiped the console with her finger, bringing up more information. "One's a heavy-load freighter and it isn't escorted, so it probably isn't carrying anything particularly valuable or dangerous."

"Weapons array?"

"A ship that size, probably a couple of laser cannons, but weapons are showing cold. If someone raided it, the crew's likelier to get in escape pods and surrender the ship, anyway."

"What about the other ships?"

"There's just one," she said. "Unidentified and three hours away."

That set off Jason's mental alarm. "Nothing about its model?"

She shook her head. "Nothing. It's a big blank. It could be their ident system isn't recognized by the *Ghost*'s systems, but I'm pretty good about keeping on top of that, so it isn't likely. They're probably cloaking it, which is why we're going to get the hell away from here as soon as possible." She sat down again at the pilot's seat and plotted a course. "We're going to head for the Pera Quadrant, which is where I wanted to go in the first place. It'll take us a day or two to get there from here, provided we don't have any more trouble."

"Where are we, exactly?"

"Quoke Quadrant," she replied. "Dead space, mostly. We're near some old commercial shipping lanes and not much else. This area doesn't even have patrols."

"That seems dangerous."

She shrugged. "This part of Bravan space is too far from the Zone to have worried about annexation. Plus, the Bravans are nice people and trust fairly easily. No one here is going to go after that freighter for scrap."

Jason knew that about the Brava System's citizens. So did the Zone, which was why they'd tried to annex sections of Bravan space for so many years. Their planets hadn't been plundered to the point of widespread poverty.

And even after repeated conflicts, the Brava System

acknowledged how badly the average Zone citizen had it and still allowed them across the border in search of a better life. He wondered how long that would last. He was surprised it had gone on as long as it had since the armistice was signed.

Cecily continued, "But there's no guarantee that the unidentified ship out there is as benevolent as that freighter or anyone else in the Brava System. Let's go."

The *Gray Ghost* jolted a little, nearly knocking Jason to the deck, but he quickly righted himself. The ship picked up speed, and smoothly glided where she belonged, among the stars in realspace.

***

Exhaustion tugged at her, but Cecily still forced herself to run a complete systems check on the *Gray Ghost*. The comp's warnings during the drop out echoed in her mind as she ran through checklists, the one about the hull in particular cause for concern.

But everything was fine: life support was fully functional, the hull hadn't taken any damage, the weapons array was as it should be. Cecily had actually managed to successfully break her ship out of subspace, and she'd done it with as much finesse as the *Ghost* could handle.

I never want to do that again. I don't think my nerves could handle it.

She looked at Jason, who was still seated next to her. He gave her a smile that, despite her tiredness, still had the power to make her blush.

Jason helped. Immensely.

She wasn't sure she would've had the courage to do such a thing if he hadn't been at her side.

I'm getting soft. I need to get the hell out of this business before I get myself killed.

"You should get some sleep," Jason said.

"I want to, but I'm afraid I'll miss something," she said.

"I shouldn't have kept you up so long."

She gave him what she hoped was her most pointed look. "Are you having regrets?"

"Of course not. But I don't need as much rest as you do. And..." He trailed off.

"What is it?"

"You nearly died, and almost as soon as you were awake, we were fucking," he said. "I feel kind of bad about that."

Cecily stared at him. "You 'kind of' feel bad about that?" It was so ridiculous that she couldn't help but laugh. "Most people 'kind of' feel bad about, I don't know, waking someone up ten minutes early, you know?" She deliberately dropped her voice to a register she hoped was seductive. "Look, don't worry about it. I think it was worth it."

He still didn't look totally convinced. Cecily tried to add a little levity to her voice, and said, "We'll find Marshall Caron sooner rather than later, and after we're fixed up, we won't have anything to worry about."

Unless he doesn't want to continue what we have when we get back to Kurkay-2.

The very notion was crushing. After having been independent for so long, without any friends or family to keep her company, she was more than ready to settle down and finally start having a normal life.

But all of that was a conversation that would have to wait until they were out of danger and their respective cybernetics repaired or replaced.

And Jason was right. She *was* tired. She'd had an amateur attempt at major surgery performed on her more recently than she'd like to remember.

She stood up. "I'm going to get a couple hours of sleep." She had to fight the urge to yawn.

Jason nodded. "Solid plan. I'll keep an eye on everything out there."

"Wake me up as soon as you notice anything," Cecily said. "No matter how insignificant."

"I will, I promise."

Cecily headed for the corridor, but before she reached it, Jason took hold of her arm. Before she could register the contact, he slanted his mouth over hers in an unexpected kiss that stole her breath away.

"Have a good sleep," he said. "Take as long as you need."

CHAPTER 11

JASON HALF-EXPECTED the unidentified ship to take chase and try to blow the *Gray Ghost* out of the star lanes. But when Cecily returned to the bridge, six and a half hours after she went to bed, everything was still normal. The ship was still on their long-range sensors and meandering along a couple of hours behind them at her current speed, but hadn't shown any signs of aggression. Yet.

She still managed to surprise and distract him a little when she kissed him good morning, then held out a mug of coffee to him. "How's everything looking?" she asked, taking her seat at the pilot's station.

"Just as it did last night. How are you feeling?"

"Wide awake and glad to be alive," Cecily replied. "And I'm planning on staying that way." She looked down at her console. "Our friend is still on our tail, and there's another subspace route nearby that he could have taken to follow us. A shorter one." She looked at that data more closely. That route had multiple entrances and exits, which would have made it easier for whoever was following them to duck in and out of subspace while they waited for the *Ghost* to resurface.

"It could be a coincidence," Jason said, even though he knew the chance was slim.

Cecily shook her head. "No way. I'm willing to make a substantial bet that whoever this is chased us into the Highland Gate to begin with." Her console lit up as she checked the *Gray Ghost*'s weapons array. "And when that Scout tracks us down, we'll be ready. The weapons array will be on standby, but I have a program that'll mask that. Traveling with hot weapons in a commercial lane is a really good way to attract unwanted attention, even if this area isn't patrolled that much." She sighed and leaned back in her seat. "I'm really hoping we won't have to have a firefight out in the open, but if I'll defend us with lethal force if necessary." She turned to him, a questioning look on her face. "Are you okay with that?"

"With what part?"

"Me killing someone."

"I've already seen you kill someone," he pointed out. "And while I would have preferred to take a crack at Garrett Jacoby myself, I still appreciate it."

Her expression relaxed a little, and he realized she was still expecting him to lash out at her. "That won't upset me," he said, trying to be as reassuring as possible. "The Scout attacked us. I'd rather be the one still alive at the end of all this. Do what you need to do." He flexed his hands. "Unfortunately, I can't help out the way Valenna's brother-in-law could, but I still have hand weapons training."

"What do you mean about Valenna's brother-in-law?"

"Lukas can electrocute people," Jason said. Lukas Best, the original cyborg, had been enhanced until he was a living weapon, and to the military's surprise, rebelled and went AWOL for a few years until he met Cressida Merchant by chance. "Through his hands. I think that's one of the reasons he always wears gloves." That, and to conceal the ports in his fingers and wrists. He had more than any of the other cyborgs.

Surprise crossed Cecily's face. "I had no idea he could do that."

"I'm sure you can see why Jacoby didn't want us to have that ability. But I'm still qualified to handle weapons," he said. "I know hand-to-hand combat. My reflexes are faster, thanks to the cybernetics."

"Oh, I don't doubt that you're a force to be reckoned with," Cecily said. "I just think that having electrocuting hands is convenient."

"It would be, but don't share that with Lukas. He's touchy about being a cyborg." He, more than any of the other surviving cyborgs, was more sensitive about his enhancements. None of them had had an easy go of it, but Lukas was especially fucked over, cybernetically speaking, when he was just a kid. He'd never had a say in how his life was supposed to go.

"I'll keep that in mind." Cecily keyed in a password sequence that Jason's enhanced vision easily picked up, and he recognized as the invasive filter she'd used to hack into the Scout's identity. He doubted the filter would work given how far behind the unidentified ship was, but he supposed there was always a chance...

He was snapped out of his ruminations when an alarm blared. Cecily slapped at the console and it shut off. "The ship's picked up speed," she announced. "It's following us."

"Holy shit."

She shook her head, a knowing smile on her face that he longed to kiss away. "No," she said. "That ship picked up our scan. It didn't confirm its ident, but it's chasing us now. It just needed a kick in the ass to catch up to us."

Jason was aghast. "You're saying that like it's a good thing."

"It *is* a good thing," she insisted. "We're pretty close to finding Marshall Caron, I can feel it. And I don't want to lead that Scout to Sidra Prime. We drag the ship out of the proverbial shadows, destroy it, and then we can carry on without too many worries about being blown out of the lanes."

Insane as the idea was, it made total sense. Jason had no doubt that when she was expecting a fight, Cecily could be formidable. Hell, even when she wasn't, she was still a force to be reckoned with. She wouldn't have survived as long as she had if she wasn't. Being taken by surprise and chased into subspace was a fluke.

Whoever was piloting the Scout was willing to launch an attack in open civilian space. Clearly, Cecily hadn't had to deal with people who played dirty before.

"So, what do we do now?" he asked.

"We're going to maintain our speed for now," she said. "We'll let the Scout catch up with us while we're still in this lane. There aren't any other ships nearby to get caught in a crossfire, but there are enough beacons to send any unauthorized combat reports to the authorities, although I'll tweak the *Ghost*'s ident codes after we annihilate the Scout."

"I like the sound of 'we,'" Jason said.

A blush colored Cecily's cheeks. "You know," she said, "so do I."

It was nearly ten in the morning when the other ship caught up to the *Gray Ghost*. To Cecily's surprise, it was the Scout.

She and Jason had already outfitted themselves with weapons from the locker near the engine room. Her Melton brainwave disruptor was strapped at one hip, and a conventional laser pistol, its charge set to kill, on the other one. Jason was similarly attired, although he'd chosen the military-grade rifle that civilians couldn't legally possess in Bravan space. Cecily supposed that she'd have to destroy it after she went straight.

And she would. She and Jason would live through this fight.

"Is it wrong that I think you look totally hot wearing that?" she asked Jason as they took their seats again on the bridge.

"The civilian side of me says yes, the military man says no. And I'm feeling the same about you right now."

Any rejoinder she could have offered him was interrupted by the trill of an incoming hail request.

She and Jason exchanged glances. Since when did would-be murderers hail before firing?

The *Gray Ghost*'s shields were active, her weapons array hot and ready to fire on a nanosecond's notice. They were well-defended; she may as well listen to whoever was trying to communicate with her.

She tabbed open the hailing frequency. "Unidentified Scout," she barked into the speaker. "What the everloving fuck is going on?"

The speaker crackled with static before a man's voice said, "I'm giving you a chance to surrender."

"Fuck you," Cecily retorted. She aimed a torpedo at the Scout.

The other pilot saw what was coming his way and responded likewise.

The command console pinged a warning. "Grade four ion torpedo," the comp voice, ever calm, announced.

Oh, shit.

A wave of dread washed over her, and Cecily thought she might be sick. "God damn it," she said. That was worse than she thought. What the hell kind of cloaking technology did that Scout have? "It's a fucking grade four!"

Before the Scout could fire on the *Ghost*, she fired her own torpedo. While it didn't totally disable the Scout, the comp told her the torpedo temporarily threw the Scout's weapons offline.

But Cecily was more concerned about "temporary." If the Scout could conceal a grade four ion torpedo from her sensors, God only knew what other tricks it had hiding in its compact body.

The Scout's image on the forward viewscreen showed a ship sharply tilted to the side, then it righted itself. The *Ghost*'s comp warned it was priming its weapons again.

Cecily fired two more torpedoes. A hole appeared in the Scout's hull.

"That's it?" Jason said, incredulous. "There's no way anyone who was on that thing could survive a hull breach."

Impulsively, Cecily threw her arms around Jason and kissed him. He eagerly returned it, tongue sweeping into her mouth and hands roving over her hips, impeded by the weapons there.

"There's a joke to be made about a gun in your pocket," she said.

A low chuckle was her only answer.

She reluctantly pulled away. "Let's pull everything we can from the Scout."

She activated her invasive filter, and unencumbered by distance and shields, data flowed into the *Ghost*'s quarantined comp banks, where any traps or viruses would be removed before she could pore over the Scout's information.

But her jubilation was short-lived when the comp voice spoke again. "Unauthorized intruder at outer hull."

"Son of a bitch," said Jason, just as Cecily yelped, "Fuck!"

"Intruder is located outside external door to the starboard cargo hold," the comp continued.

"Any ident chips?" Cecily asked. Her mind raced, trying to decide what to do next. She hadn't planned on anyone being tenacious or stupid enough to abandon ship and then attach himself to a hull's cargo door.

"None that can be verified at this time."

"How is he alive?" she grumbled as she dashed away from the bridge, Jason following.

"Sensors indicate the intruder is wearing a high-speed EVA suit."

"Damn it," Cecily said. The EVA suits propelled themselves for short distances, ideal in emergency situations if there was a ship nearby for rescue. She never used them. They could only keep their wearers alive for little more than an hour. Escape pods were the preferred evacuation method for anyone with a shred of sense.

They clattered down the stairs to the airlock. As if he could read her mind, Jason said, "At least he only has an hour or two worth of air, tops."

"Yeah, but I doubt he's planning on hanging off my door until it runs out," she said. "He probably has something to use to break in."

"Intruder has initiated usage of a thermo-file," the comp said.

"See?" said Cecily. "I'm going to go out there, kill him, and you'll let me back in."

"What? No. I'll go out there. Out of the two of us, I'm better suited for hand-to-hand combat," Jason protested.

Cecily opened a storage locker and pulled out her EVA suit. "This won't fit you," she said. "And I only have one. The alternative is to let him break through my cargo door and destroy that part of the ship before he tries to kill us. I'm going to go out there, take him by surprise, and kill him." She narrowed her eyes at him. "You're forgetting that I'm good at hand-to-hand combat, too. And I fight dirty. You have to, when most of your opponents are men."

She didn't wait for Jason to protest that and stepped into her suit. God bless him, he didn't argue, but instead helped her check to make sure it was sealed and its life support online.

She strapped her Melton and pistol to her hips. "We'll be in constant contact," she said, helmet in her hands. "I think I'm ready to go out there."

Before she could put it over her head, he kissed her. "*Now* you're ready."

She smiled, her heart fluttering. The stupid thing better hold up until they were done here.

She fitted the helmet over her head and sealed it. "You'll be okay to let me out and seal the airlock again?" she asked.

He sounded far away through the helmet's speakers. "Yeah, I've downloaded everything," he said, tapping his head. "Come back here alive, okay?"

"Of course."

A surge of emotion welled inside her, and she turned away to face the airlock door before Jason could see it and think she was unable to complete the unpleasant task before her. Squaring her shoulders, she waited until Jason closed the airlock accessway's door and the airlock safety lights glowed green.

She activated the magnetic hold on her boots and gloves and unsealed the door.

Cecily disliked spacewalks, and knowing she had to kill someone made this one all the more odious. After the airlock door closed again, she scaled the *Ghost*'s hull, up toward the ship's oblong top, hoping whoever the intruder was couldn't hear her footsteps. For the first time, she was glad she'd paid extra to have her EVA suit's boots outfitted with muffling technology.

Not that being quiet would save her if the high-speed EVA suit the intruder was wearing could sense her, but she'd worry about that when they met face-to-face.

Once on the top of the ship, she lumbered across the roof, wanting to take the intruder by surprise. Jason's voice crackled through the speaker. "You're on the roof?"

"Yeah."

"I can see you on the specs," he said. "Keep walking straight ahead. The cargo door is a straight shot down."

She grinned. "Thank you."

"Stay safe out there."

His faith in her bolstered her wavering confidence in herself.

She could do this. She could do one last hit, in some of the worst circumstances she'd ever worked, and come out of it alive.

She peered over the edge of the ship, Melton in hand. *Thank God I sprang for a brainwave disruptor that works in zero-g.*

To think that Anders considered her ship, her supplies, unnecessarily extravagant. *I'm not all about velvet-covered pilot's seats, and I'll tell him that the next time I see him.*

And she *would* see him again. She'd make up with him, too.

The intruder was intently aiming a thermo-file at her starboard cargo bay door. A descrambler was attached to the lock, its indicator light glowing red for its denied access. Cecily smiled. At least her locking mechanisms were secure.

She aimed her Melton at the intruder. In that instant, he looked up.

He glowed a little in the light offered by his suit's helmet, and his features were unfamiliar to Cecily. She couldn't hear him, but he mouthed what looked like, "What the hell?"

Cecily activated the Melton on its highest setting. His

helmet cracked, and she saw the horror on his face as he realized what was happening. A second later, its plastiglas sheared apart.

She closed her eyes, not wanting to see him as he died.

At least it was quick.

Quick, terrifying, and undoubtedly painful.

He was going to kill me first. But I never want to do that again.

She took a deep breath, fortifying herself.

"Everything okay?" Jason asked. "The comp recorded a fatality."

"It isn't me."

"That's why I'm not freaking out. It was an unidentified fatality."

"Yeah," she said. "He's dead." She forced herself to look over the ship's edge.

He was still crouched against the hull, mag boots stuck to the side. He'd let go of the thermo-file in death, and it had long since floated away.

His helmet was in pieces, his exposed head... Cecily gulped. His eyes were wide open and bulging from their sockets, his skin already flaking away in space's vacuum. His mouth gaped open in a final, silent scream.

It was the first time Cecily killed someone and she thought she might puke after. Even though he'd been dispatched to kill her, she regretted that the Melton hadn't been able to penetrate his helmet more effectively, making his death faster and less painful. It took less than two minutes to die in open space, but she knew they had to be the longest two minutes in the universe.

She crawled down the ship's side and pried his body off the hull with one of the tools still strapped around his waist. It took more effort than she expected and she was sweating in her EVA suit when she was done, but he finally floated away. She would have to fire on him, make sure his body was destroyed before they resumed their search for Marshall Caron. Any beacons around the *Ghost* would have detected the use of firepower by now and alerted the transit authorities; she didn't want them to trace the Scout or its pilot to her.

The damage to the cargo door was superficial. His thermo-file wasn't powerful enough for her reinforced hull. At least that was a relief.

She activated her comm link to Jason. "I'm coming back in."

There was a haunted look on Cecily's face when she stripped off her EVA suit. The airlock accessway was freezing, even to Jason, and she was shivering when she returned the suit to its locker.

When she wordlessly hugged him, still trembling, he knew it wasn't entirely due to the accessway's chill.

"He asphyxiated," she said into his neck.

What a horrible way to die. He tightened his hold on her.

"I like to make it as fast as I can," she said. "He still had to die, but I didn't want to be a sadist."

He kissed the top of her hair, wishing he had reassuring words for her.

After a moment, he said, "The Scout's data is out of quarantine."

She pulled away, the haunted look still there. "Oh?"

"The pilot's name was Robert Winters. Dishonorably discharged from the Zone military four years ago, had a criminal record as long as my arm. The Scout was the property of Wilton Intergalactic Fluid Technology. They're a water seller based in the Zone and looking to expand into the Brava System."

Cecily immediately understood what he was saying. "The water company wants cybernetic slaves."

Jason nodded. "That's what I would guess, too. If a cyborg's brain and body are re-wired just right, they could become totally incapable of independent thought or action. Winters was hired to steal the technology you have on your ship, kill you, and maybe even get me as an added bonus for study."

"Anders can breathe underwater," Cecily said. Alarm flashed across her face. "We have to get in touch with him and tell him to get the hell away from his homestead. He has to hide out somewhere."

"I'm sure he'll be okay, but..."

"No, he and Valenna need to go into hiding." Cecily pushed past him and he followed. "We'll get a warning out to him and Rordan Alexander, and then we'll find Marshall Caron. We need to get the hell out of here before any transit authority ships show up, anyway." Something else struck her. "WIFT. Wilton Intergalactic Fluid Technology. That's the code name in the data we pulled from the Scout."

Jason didn't look surprised to hear that. He'd probably already figured it out for himself.

She sat down in the pilot's seat, and Jason took copilot. She activated the bridge's visualizer, smiling into the screen. "Hey, big brother," she began. "I have some news for you."

CHAPTER 12

PRINCESS CAY!

Cecily stared at the words on the command console, hardly daring to believe it.

Marshall Caron's been living in Princess Cay on Sidra Prime all this time. A goddamn tropical getaway!

At least the visit there would be pleasant. It would be nice to feel real sun on her face. In another lifetime, maybe she could return and lie on one of its legendary beaches. The real thing had to be so much better than what the ship's systems conjured in the sim chamber.

Now that she was in deep Bravan space, the firefight in the space lanes a day behind her and Jason, her research became easier as smaller, more obscure packets of the galactic net became available. She was finally able to pinpoint Marshall Caron's last known whereabouts and she was sure he was still there. She'd even found a holo of him on a beach with a young woman who bore a striking resemblance to him.

From the news reports she'd gathered, local to Sidra Prime, it seemed Dr. Caron was something of a celebrity. He was universally regarded as kind and generous, popular with the native Sidrans. There was no mention that she could find of his previous career in cybernetics and it appeared he presented himself as a semi-retired pediatrician. He had been, of sorts. Lukas Best started his cyborg surgeries when he was a kid at the cybernetics research facility that bore Dr. Caron's name.

A spaceport a few kilometers away from Princess Cay authorized the *Gray Ghost*'s landing and dry dock space in the early afternoon. Cecily had worried about being caught by Bravan authorities for the firefight, but no one had contacted her, and the incident hadn't even made it to the news broadcasts. It looked like she and Jason had done very well in covering it up. All that was left of the Scout and Winters were particles smaller than the grains of sand on Princess Cay's beaches.

Cecily rented an antigrav flitter at the spaceport, not wanting to take the public shuttle to Princess Cay proper. She and Jason, dressed in lighter clothes more suitable to the beach, climbed aboard the flitter, hand weapons concealed in a duffel, just in case. Jason had a data drive in his pocket, holding every scrap of information about cyborgs.

Neither spoke much as the flitter noiselessly zipped above the ground, which gradually shifted from pavement to grass to golden sand. While Jason guided the flitter, Cecily leaned back, eyes closed, basking in the sensation of sunlight on her face for the first time in... she thought back to the last time she had the chance to enjoy a real sun and came up blank.

It was a nice way to forget everything for a few minutes. Hell, she might even get a chance to dip her toes in a real ocean. She wasn't wearing her black bikini under her shorts and tank top just to look like she belonged in the crowd of beach-goers, nor were the towels in the duffel there only to conceal the Melton and laser pistol.

"What are you thinking?" Jason asked. She heard the smile in his voice.

"I'm wondering if the ocean is as cold as I've read it is."

"Don't think of it as cold, think of it as refreshing."

"That's a very glass-is-half-full way to look at it." She opened her eyes and turned her head to face him. "You actually look relaxed."

"How can I not?" Keeping one hand on the flitter's controls, he gestured with the other. "Look at this place. No wonder Caron moved here. I'd never want to leave."

"Are you reconsidering returning to Kurkay-2?"

"I'm not going to lie, this place is beautiful and already established. I wouldn't have to mulch leaves. But it's probably way too expensive."

Jason wasn't a poor man; at least, he wasn't since he was rescued from Omega-Three-Omega and his bank account topped up with Cecily and Serena Glazer's know-how. The funds were plundered from Garrett Jacoby and Colton Byers' accounts. At the thought of the female cyborg, the most sophisticated model in existence, Cecily smiled again. She would love this place.

Cecily wasn't poor, either. Neither were Anders and Valenna, who'd both made their preferences for living a quiet, simple life well-known.

She and Jason could return here, if they wanted. Sidra Prime was an expensive planet, but still manageable for them.

If he wanted to live here or be with her at all after this was over.

Her heart clenched in a way that had nothing to do with her cybernetics at the thought of their parting.

"You look like you smelled something bad," Jason said.

Cecily rearranged her expression. "I didn't. Just thinking."

"About what?"

She paused, considering what to say next.

May as well be honest. We're either having major surgery, or we're going to die. Or both.

"I like you," she said.

Confusion shadowed his face. "Okay. I like you, too. I thought we established that a couple of days ago."

"What happens after this?" she asked.

"You said you wanted to go straight," Jason replied. "I figured I'd go back to Anders and Valenna's farm. I have nowhere else to be."

"No," she said. "I mean, us."

She'd never had that conversation before in her twenty-four years. She had no idea if she was doing it correctly.

"I don't know," he said. "I've never had a serious girlfriend before."

She waited for him to continue, not wanting to break his train of thought.

"Have you had a serious relationship?" he finally asked.

"No."

"So, we're equally clueless." He had a smile on his face.

"Oh, my God." Frustration and hope warred within her. "Are you saying you want to try to have a normal relationship after this is over?"

"I think we deserve a vacation first, but yes."

"Okay."

"That's it?" he said. "'Okay'?"

"It's not like we can have celebratory sex on the beach right away, so it'll have to do for now," she said. Thinking of what lay ahead for them, she said, "Damn it, we should have had sex again while we still had the chance."

"I'll have to make sure not to die on the operating table, then."

"Please don't make jokes about that."

"It'll be the first and last one," Jason said. "I promise."

With his free hand, he affectionately squeezed Cecily's thigh. She leaned back in her seat and tried to enjoy the feel of the sun on her face again.

The golden beach stretched further than Jason thought it would, pristine blue ocean water lapping at the sandbar. Scores of people sunned themselves on towels, others sat under huge umbrellas. Locals walked up and down an old-fashioned boardwalk with nary a care in the world. It looked to be as low-tech as Renza was, but the people here seemed happy, unencumbered by religion and self-imposed misery. It was the nicest place he'd ever been to, and he could see why Marshall Caron chose to retire here.

He and Jason secured the flitter, and he draped their duffel over his shoulder, not wanting to leave the weapons behind. He saw Cecily look at the beach longingly, and reached for her hand, lacing his fingers through hers. "Maybe later," he said, inclining his head to the water.

"Yeah, maybe," she echoed, but there was doubt there.

He felt it, too. What if Marshall Caron had taken off? What if he refused to help them?

His last known address was near the beach, and they walked along Princess Cay's meandering stone-paved streets. Some homes were built on the ground, others in trees, and all were unique and magnificent: a mix of ultra-modern, boxy plastiglas houses reminiscent of Center City's wealthier suburbs and miniature castles straight out of children's fairy tales. Jason thought he probably could have spent a couple of hours just gawking at the houses.

"Up there," Cecily said, pointing.

Jason looked up, his ocular enhancements automatically darkening to protect his eyes against the sun. A tree stretched up toward it, at least six meters, a house perched in its branches. Winding around the trunk was a staircase leading up to it. Nailed to the railing was a sign that read *CARON SANCTUARY*.

And all of it, completely unguarded. At least to his eyes and sensors, which had also picked up humanoid heat signatures, two of them.

"I think the good doctor's home," he said. Without relinquishing his hold on Cecily's hand, they began their ascent up the staircase. The steps were decorated with pots of brightly-colored flowers and chunks of pink rock that sparkled in the sun.

"This seems too easy," Cecily said.

"Are you going to tell me that getting chased into subspace and getting into a firefight in a commercial space lane is *easy*?"

"You know what I mean," she said. "I expected more, I don't know, firepower. Less cheerful trinkets on stairs leading to a treehouse. I can't remember the last time I went somewhere that was this welcoming." She looked up. "I think I want to live in a treehouse."

Jason could see the appeal. Everything he'd seen so far indicated that he'd probably be very happy whiling away the rest of his days on Sidra Prime.

The landing was adorned with more flowerpots and a polished gray stone bench, its surface marbled with black veins. The front door was made of heavy wood, inset with a plastiglas window, its biometric locks the only trace of modernity Jason had seen so far.

He and Cecily exchanged glances, and he knocked on the door and waited.

A moment later, it opened, revealing a woman he recognized from the holo Cecily showed him aboard the *Ghost*. She looked to be in her mid to late twenties, a couple of years older than him and Cecily. She was tanned, her dark hair streaked from being bleached by the sun. "Hi," she said. "Can I help you?"

Cecily nodded. "We're looking for Dr. Marshall Caron."

"Oh, of course." She stepped inside, gesturing for them to

move into the foyer. "Is it that cold that's been going around the crèches? Keep the kids hydrated and they'll be fine in a day or two."

"Uh, not quite," Jason said.

"Let me get him," she said. Then, over her shoulder, she called, "Dad! Company!"

Jason looked at Cecily, saw the incredulous look on her face and knew his expression had to be mirroring hers.

A tall, gray-haired man walked into the foyer. "What can I help you with?" he asked brightly. "I..."

His voice faded as he took in Jason, and he took a small step back without saying another word.

His daughter looked between them, confusion and fear in her eyes. "Dad?" she said cautiously. "What's going on?"

Without taking his gaze off Jason, Dr. Caron said, "I don't know. But I do know a cyborg's eyes when I see them."

"*What*?" his daughter gasped.

"We're here for your help," Cecily said. "We've come a long way, and we're both in trouble. All of our research shows that you're probably the only person in the universe who can help us."

Dr. Caron blinked at each of them, as if he couldn't decide he believed her words. "So, you're not here to kill me," he said to Jason. His daughter let out a small cry of fright.

"Not at all," Jason said. "But I have something in my head that might kill me."

"And I have a cybernetic heart," Cecily said. "It's failing."

"Well, that's a relief," Dr. Caron said, shoulders slumping. "Not about your troubles, but that you're not out for my blood." To his daughter, he said, "Dasha, could you fix us a pitcher of iced tea and bring it to the living room? Some of those fruit biscuits, too."

Her gaze flicked back and forth between them and her father. "Are you sure?"

"It's fine, sweetheart. If this gentleman wanted to kill me, he'd have done it already." He straightened. "Forgive me, I don't even know your names."

"Jason Formosa, former captain with the Zone military. This is Cecily Barris."

"Well, you know I'm Marshall Caron," the doctor said. "The scowling young lady here is my daughter, Dasha."

His daughter rolled her eyes and left the foyer. Dr. Caron smiled.

"Let's sit down and have a talk," he said. "And I'll see what I can do about your ailments."

Dr. Caron's eyes darted back and forth over his thincomp, now loaded with everything Cecily and Jason downloaded into the data drive. Occasionally, his eyes would widen and he cursed under his breath in Branta.

Jason and Cecily sat side-by-side on a well-worn couch, sipping iced tea and nibbling on homemade fruit biscuits. Cecily didn't know what kind of fruit they were made with, but the treats were delicious.

As Dr. Caron read, she took in what she'd seen of the treehouse so far. A staircase extended to the second level at the opposite end of the living room. Big windows all around the space let light flood in, tempered by the leaves of the house's tree. The furniture was heavy and expensive-looking but well-loved, and the couch she shared with Jason had a homemade quilt draped over its back. Holos of Dr. Caron, Dasha, and a woman Cecily presumed to be Dasha's mother decorated the walls, interspersed with artwork from all over the galaxy.

It was a cozy home, the kind Cecily never had and always wanted.

Dasha joined them, sitting down on an easy chair next to

the one Dr. Caron occupied. All traces of suspicion disappeared from her face, replaced with curiosity and, Cecily guessed, anticipation.

Dr. Caron set the thincomp aside and rubbed his eyes. "I told those fools not to continue with the cyborg program," he said. "It was inhumane." To Jason, he said, "You're acquainted with Lukas Best?"

Jason nodded. "We've met."

"I will never forgive myself for my part in what was done to him," Dr. Caron said. "I founded the cybernetics facility as a way to introduce lower-cost replacements for body parts to people who otherwise couldn't afford a new kidney or who'd had their arms blown off during the war. I'm sure you aware that once you're discharged from the military, no matter the reason, you're on your own."

"Yes."

To Cecily, Dr. Caron said, "You were exactly the kind of patient I envisioned, but this excuse for a heart shouldn't have been implanted in you. I designed organs that were meant to be used indefinitely. Gara-Holt's bastardization was a money grab." He looked away, fixating on the antique glass-topped coffee table separating them, and clenched his jaw. Cecily had the distinct impression that he was fighting the urge to put his fist through it in frustration. "Planned obsolescence has no place in medicine.

"I didn't even patent the parts I designed," he continued. "I wanted them to be inexpensive and widely available. It looks like my design was copied, deliberately botched, and implanted in vulnerable patients with the intent of forcing them to buy new organs every few years."

"Dad," said Dasha, but Dr. Caron cut her off.

"This wasn't supposed to happen!" he roared and tossed the thincomp on the coffee table with a bang. Everyone else in the room jumped.

"Why did you get involved in the military's cyborg project?" Jason asked, voice level.

The doctor breathed deeply, centering himself, Cecily thought. "Caron Cybernetics was originally contracted to develop artificial limbs for wounded soldiers," he replied. "It was a financial boon to the company. Then the military's researchers and doctors moved in and started changing the course of my research, and the original aims of the company were tossed by the wayside like a pile of space junk." He looked squarely at Jason, then Cecily, who suppressed a shiver under the intensity of his gaze. "I did not condone what happened to Lukas Best at any point in his enhancement surgery, nor did I supervise any of those surgeries. I was in the lab most of the time, working on organs."

"It was your company," Cecily said quietly.

"In name only. Admiral Stephen Best—I suppose you know he's Lukas's father—moved in his own people as soon as he could. He'd been watching my research for years. I have no doubt the reason Lukas exists is so he could be turned into a super-soldier." He paused. "After I defected to the Brava System, I cut ties with everyone involved in the project for my own safety and that of Dasha. What happened to him?"

"He went AWOL," said Jason. "Holed himself up in an abandoned military installation on a backwater planet for a few years, living off the local flora and military rations left behind. He lives in Center City on Echo-7 now with his girlfriend. He doesn't talk about his experiences in the military that much."

"Or at all," Cecily added. "He's a quiet sort."

"But he's sane?" Dr. Caron asked. "You mentioned a girlfriend?"

"Yeah, Cressida," Cecily said. "She's actually the sister of my brother's partner, and my brother's a cyborg, too."

"The fellow who was kept underwater, according to your

notes," Dr. Caron said. "I'm not a religious man, but if there's any justice in the universe, everyone who furthered that research the way they did should be rotting in hell."

"Garrett Jacoby and Colton Byers are dead," Jason said. "Cecily killed Jacoby herself."

"Is that so?" Dr. Caron raised a bushy eyebrow in Cecily's direction. "He was always a pompous prick. Good riddance."

"There's something else," Cecily said. "That wasn't on the data drive. While we were on our way here, we were chased into subspace by a thug hired by Wilton Intergalactic Fluids Technology. I, uh, neutralized him, but we have reason to believe people are after this technology. And people are after you, too."

He didn't seem surprised to find that out. "Of course, they would be," Dr. Caron said. "I'm sure they want it for the same reason the military wanted it: to create mindless drones. If that's the case, your friends still in the Zone need to get out. The Bravans' generous open border policy won't last forever." He leaned forward. "I don't think the war's really over, either. The Zone won't be happy until it's annexed half of Bravan space and done to it what it did to their own territory and people."

Something in Cecily twisted itself, painfully, when she thought of Lukas and Cressida. And what about Serena Glazer and Matthias Ericks? They spent their time running Matthias's shipping business in the Zone's Rim Worlds and lived on a freighter. Serena's nanobots were deactivated and her cybernetic functions muted, but she was still technically a cyborg, and the only female one in the galaxy at that.

"But you aren't here to talk about war," Dr. Caron said. "You're here for surgery, am I correct?"

"You were the only person we could think who might know what to do," Cecily said. "Jason can't be treated by any other doctor and I don't trust anyone."

"You're in luck, in that I can help you," Dr. Caron said.

Cecily couldn't keep a squeal of excitement from escaping her. She clapped her hand over her mouth, and Jason gave her a smile.

"Jason's surgery is fairly straightforward," Dr. Caron said. "I see Jacoby constructed the brain enhancements in a way that I explicitly advised against, for obvious reasons. There was another man who has the same kill switch according to this documentation. Rordan Alexander. Where is he?"

Jason glanced at her, and she sighed, dreading her next words. "We don't know."

Dasha finally spoke. "Oh?"

"He asked me to leave him at Spaceport 44 after we rescued them from Omega-Three-Omega," Cecily said.

"He didn't want to keep in touch with any of us," Jason said.

"We weren't sure what to do," Cecily said. "So, we decided to look for you first."

But he surprised her when he didn't look on her with judgement, and his voice remained understanding. "Well, when the ship's under an evacuation order, get yourself into an escape pod first," Dr. Caron said. "That was a truly untenable situation to be in. But I'm sure you realize that you must find him as soon as possible."

Cecily nodded, but she wasn't sure how to find a cyborg who didn't want to be found. She'd tried, repeatedly, and knew Serena had, too. Rordan Alexander may as well have dropped off the edge of the universe for all she knew.

"But enough talk," Dr. Caron said. He stood up. "I have a small practice further in town. I'll be able to perform Jason's adjustment there, and I'll schedule Cecily for a heart transplant tomorrow morning."

It took a few seconds for the doctor's words to sink in, and longer for her to find her voice. "You can do a heart transplant," she said flatly. "Tomorrow."

He nodded. "I have the appropriate devices available here. But there's still standard surgery procedures to be followed. Your stomach will have to be completely empty, so you can't eat or drink anything after midnight tonight. Your medical records show that the original transplant was performed correctly and you don't have any significant scar tissue, which makes my job much easier, so I don't anticipate any complications."

Tears pricked at Cecily's eyes, and she brushed them away impatiently. When she glanced at Jason, she saw he looked as shocked as she felt. "How do I repay you?" she asked. "What do you want?"

"When you leave Sidra Prime, you're going to take us with you," Dr. Caron said.

"*What*?" exclaimed Dasha. "Dad, what the hell?"

"If corporate thugs are after cyborg technology, they'll track me down eventually," Dr. Caron said. "They won't harm hesitate to harm either of us to get what they want."

"Dad, you can't be serious," Dasha protested.

"I am. I have the ability and means to protect my home and practice, but I can't keep my eye on you all the time," Dr. Caron said firmly to her. "We both know that if anyone wants to get to me, you're my weakness. And I want you away from Sidra Prime until this is over." To Cecily and Jason, he said, "Keep us away from the Zone. We're never going back there. I wouldn't be surprised if our ident chips are flagged in their systems."

"Most of us are living on Kurkay-2," Jason said. "You'll be safe there."

"Kurkay-2?" yelped Dasha. "That's so far! Are you crazy?"

"It's as good a place as any," Dr. Caron said. He slanted a look at Dasha.

He stood up, gathering his thincomp. "Dasha, could you take Cecily to the guest room? Maybe you two would like to go to the beach while I take Jason for his procedure?"

"You say it like it's a routine thing," Cecily said.

"For me, it is," Dr. Caron replied. "I designed his brain enhancements. Granted, they were originally created to ease epilepsy symptoms and minimize brain damage following cancer surgery or injuries, but the kill switch can easily be disabled, if not removed."

"Do you want me to go with you?" Cecily asked Jason.

Jason's gaze flickered between her and Dr. Caron. "I'll be okay," he said quietly. "I promise. I trust him."

"So do I, but it's your *brain*," she said urgently.

"And the man who invented my enhancements is going to fix it," he said. He laced his fingers through hers. "I'll be back soon."

"A couple of hours," Dr. Caron said. "He'll want to sleep afterwards, but that's to be expected after brain surgery."

"Go to the beach," Jason said. "You've always wanted to go to a real one, haven't you?"

Tears spilled down her cheeks, but she nodded.

"Go and have fun," Jason said. His fingers traced her tears' path. "I'll be back before you know it."

"All right," she said. Then, not heeding that other people were in the room, she took his face in her hands and kissed him hungrily, desperately hoping she wasn't about to make a huge mistake, that she would never see him alive again.

I love you, she nearly said, but stopped herself. She didn't want to say that for the first time in front of an audience, and waiting would give her something to look forward to.

Jason pulled away, and both stood up. To Dr. Caron, he said, "Let's do this."

CHAPTER 13

THE THRILL of finally feeling hot sand under her bare feet was greatly tempered by the knowledge that Jason was currently undergoing brain surgery. While Cecily appreciated Dasha's efforts to distract her, her mind kept drifting back to all the things that could go wrong.

Plus, he wasn't here to enjoy the beach with her.

It should be Jason at her side, walking hand-in-hand in the surf. She should be squealing in shock at the feel of ice-cold ocean water lapping at her ankles as Jason laughed.

At least Dasha seemed understanding at Cecily's reluctance to enjoy the beach. She set up a large umbrella on the sand and settled underneath it on a large towel, watching the waves as Cecily tried to enjoy them.

Cecily didn't last long in the water and finally sat down next to Dasha on one of the towels she'd brought with her. She remembered the weapons stashed in the duffel and felt like an idiot now. Sidra Prime wasn't known for violence. Why would Dr. Caron settle here if he was a violent man?

"Jason will be okay, you know," said Dasha without preamble.

"That's what I keep telling myself."

"My dad's a great doctor."

"I know."

"He never talked that much about what he did in the Zone," Dasha continued.

"Oh?" Cecily tilted her head to the side, wanting to hear more.

"He's an idealist," Dasha said. "He's brilliant, but have you ever met brilliant people who are completely naive to how the rest of the universe works? I've noticed that it's common in academia and other high-level careers."

"I can't say I have." Lowering her voice, Cecily said, "I'm... kind of a mercenary, I guess. For now. I'm giving it up for good after my heart's fixed."

Dasha seemed unfazed to hear that. "I guessed as much when you said you killed that doctor who turned Jason into a cyborg. I'm sure you have interesting stories. None of which involve naive people."

"No."

"But like I was saying, Dad's almost too kind for his own good," Dasha said. "He really believed that starting his own cybernetics research facility was a good idea. That the technology he developed would only be used for poor people who need new lungs or whatever and couldn't afford an organic transplant, and soldiers returning home from war would get their new limbs."

"That *does* sound naive."

"Yeah. He was always angry that the tech with his name on it was used to transform a kid into a cyborg." Dasha's eyes searched Cecily's face. "You know him?"

"Yes."

"And he's really okay? You weren't just saying that for the benefit of my father?"

"I don't know him well, but as far as I know, he's all right. About as good as you can expect from a cyborg who went into self-imposed exile for a few years." She shrugged. "He's devoted to his partner, and she's just as devoted to him. They seem happy."

"If that's true, my dad will be very glad to know that."

"I have no reason to lie."

"So, you'll tell me the truth when I ask about the weapons you have in your bag?"

Cecily slanted a glance at her, internal alarms flaring. "What?"

"We're not completely defenseless. Our door sensors picked them up when you walked into our house." Dasha surprised Cecily with a smile. "I'm not mad. I had a spanner in my back pocket the whole time. Worst case scenario, I would've induced an EMP through the whole house."

Cecily stared at her, aghast. She wouldn't have expected someone like Dasha to be that, well... a little like herself.

"You wouldn't happen to be a mercenary, would you?" she asked.

"No, just prepared. The original cyborg showing up and taking his revenge on Dad was always in the back of my mind," she said. "I'm happy to hear that he isn't likely to go on a murderous rampage."

"He ran away from the military precisely because he was sick of rampages. And the EMP is a nice touch," Cecily added. "You've also managed to scare the shit out of me, considering I have some of that same hardware in my chest."

"You wouldn't be incapacitated that long."

"No shit. I'd probably be dead."

Dasha laughed, and even though she was still worried about Jason, terrified of what their futures could hold, Cecily joined her.

Finally, when their mirth ended, Cecily said, "You never answered me. Are you a mercenary?"

"No."

"Assassin?"

"That's just a mercenary's real job title, and no."

Cecily racked her brain. "Doctor? Medic?"

"No to both. I'm a teacher, believe it or not."

"I don't."

Dasha nodded. "It's true. I teach primary school, year one. And I read a lot of adventure novels on the side."

"So, you spend your days with a bunch of six-year-olds," Cecily said. "Are you *sure* you would've known what to do with that spanner?"

"I would've thrown it at you and hoped for the best," Dasha said. "Although the electromagnetic pulse would've been a better defense. I'm glad I didn't have to use it." She sighed. "Teaching isn't the career I dreamed about, but I like the kids and the money's good in a place like Princess Cay. The kids are well-behaved, at least. For the most part."

"Are you going to miss it when you and your dad leave Sidra Prime?"

Dasha's expression softened. "A little. But I'm always keen to go to new places. I haven't been able to travel as much as I would've liked. Dad was too paranoid about my safety, and after my mother passed away, lonely." Before Cecily could ask anything more, she added, "Shuttle accident. A real one, not a staged one from the Zone military or government."

"I'm sorry. My parents also died in an accident."

"Never trust cheap, Zone-built conveyances," Dasha said. She looked at the water. "Do you know how to swim?"

"Not really."

"Then don't go in too deep." She stood up. "Let's check out the water."

Dr. Caron's clinic was smaller than Jason expected, but spotlessly clean. He was more comfortable than he thought he'd be when he lay down on the exam table.

"This will be straightforward," Dr. Caron said. He dipped his hands in a round metal container. When he lifted them, Jason saw they were coated in a blue-colored glove solution: sterile, but allowing his hands to remain as dexterous as possible for the surgery. "Jacoby's notes were very thorough, and he didn't deviate too much from my original blueprints for what's in your head. I won't be going into this blind."

"I can't tell you how relieved I am to hear that."

A metallic arm descended from a port in the ceiling and pressed a sedative patch to Jason's neck. He felt sleepy almost immediately. "How long?" he asked, fighting to keep his eyes open.

"Maybe an hour," Dr. Caron replied cheerfully. "You'll be out of here soon enough, and then I'll operate on Cecily in the morning."

"Don't let anything bad happen to her." Jason gave up and let his eyes drift shut.

"I wouldn't dream of it."

That was good, because he still needed to tell her he loved her.

———

"Jason?"

He stirred, but his head pounded so hard he could hardly move. When he tried to blink, the lights hurt his eyes. "Mmm?" was all he could manage.

"It worked. The surgery was a complete success."

"Mmm?" He finally registered the voice as belonging to Dr. Caron.

"Your kill switch was deactivated. I couldn't remove it completely, but it doesn't work anymore."

"Mmm." He finally forced his eyes open, then covered them with his arm when the light was too much to tolerate. It felt much heavier than it was supposed to.

"Silly me. I apologize." The lights dimmed a few seconds later. "How's that?"

Jason could finally form words. "Much better. Thank you." His voice sounded rougher than usual. "The surgery worked?"

"Perfectly. You're a very healthy man, Mr. Formosa."

A smile tugged at the corners of his mouth at being referred to a man instead of a machine. Cecily had done as much, too. He needed that affirmation.

"It'll take a couple of hours for you to fully recover," Dr. Caron said. "I don't expect you'll have any complications. Just take it easy for the next few days."

Jason swallowed. *I need some water.* "Can I swim?"

"Beg your pardon?"

"Swimming," he said. "Cecily always wanted to go to a real beach, and now that we're here ..." He coughed and tried to sit up. Tried, failed, and settled for rolling on his side. "Well, there's a perfectly good beach and ocean."

Dr. Caron pressed a bottle of water in his hand. "Do you know how?"

"Not really, but I figured I'd just wade in the water a little." He pried off the lid and took a grateful sip.

"If Cecily's up for it after her heart surgery, I don't see why not. Just don't overextend yourselves."

Did sex count as overextending themselves? Jason was too embarrassed to ask.

"I need you two healthy to get us away from Sidra Prime," Dr. Caron said. "Neither Dasha nor I know how to fly a ship, although I'm sure Dasha's eager to learn how to handle something bigger than a shuttle." He thought for a few seconds. "If not eager to leave Sidra Prime altogether. She's always had an adventurous streak she couldn't indulge much here."

"Kurkay-2 won't be what you're used to," Jason warned him. "It's nice, but there's a lot of rain."

"I'm sure it'll be fine," Dr. Caron replied. "I've worked in the trenches. Kurkay-2 is still better than anything else in the Zone. And speaking of the Zone, we must find that unaccounted-for cyborg as soon as possible."

"He didn't want to be found. He didn't want to have anything to do with us." Sadness pulled at Jason at the memory of Rordan Alexander. "He might already be dead."

"I doubt that," Dr. Caron said. "If nothing else, you and Cecily would have found out about that now by now. You have those connections."

He didn't, but Cecily certainly did. And Dr. Caron was right: if Rordan was dead, the news would've hit the darker parts of the galactic net. Dead cyborgs were bound to be worth hundreds of thousands or millions of scrip on the black market.

Fortified by the water and the sure knowledge that he no longer had a ticking time bomb in his head, Jason finally hauled himself to a seated position. "How soon do you think we'll be able to travel?" he asked.

Dr. Caron shrugged. "Three, four days after I've operated on Cecily. That'll also give me enough time to wrap things up here and pass the practice along to the new doctor. Everyone here has been waiting for me to fully retire, anyway."

"Won't that seem suspicious?" Jason asked. "Just packing up and getting the hell out of Princess Cay?"

"Not particularly. Everyone knows I had a life in the Zone before I moved here. They don't know the details, but they'll be understanding. Now, do you need a hoverchair, or are you all right to walk on your own?"

Jason swung his legs over the side of the bed. He already felt better, less like he'd been jettisoned into open space.

He remembered Robert Winters and the gruesome way he died. *Bad analogy.* He shuddered.

He was a little unsteady when his feet touched the floor, but he regained enough equilibrium to walk without help. "I think I'll be okay to make it out of here on my own," he said.

Dr. Caron beamed. "Excellent. Let's get you in the flitter and back to my home. Fresh air is always helpful in recovery."

***

Cecily couldn't sleep.

It wasn't just because she was hungry and thirsty and she had to wait until after her heart surgery in the morning to eat and drink. Since Jason was in bed next to her, breathing deeply in sleep and his kill switch deactivated, it wasn't that, either.

She wasn't afraid of the surgery being botched. She'd survived a black market heart transplant and its restarting by a cyborg with no medical training; she'd live through a proper transplant in a licensed clinic.

She sat up in bed. Shadows danced across the darkened room from the tree branches swaying in a gentle breeze. Salt air drifted inside from the beach, and a fierce longing to be outside crashed into her with as much force as the ocean's waves.

Night swimming wasn't safe, but it wouldn't hurt to walk along the sandbar for a little while. Just long enough to feel tired again.

But when her feet touched the cool floor, Jason whispered, "Cecily?"

She immediately turned to him. "Are you okay?"

"Yeah. Are you?"

He hadn't spoken much since he arrived back at the Carons' treehouse in the afternoon. He'd lasted all of fifteen minutes before announcing that he needed some sleep, and he'd been passed out in the guest room ever since. "I'm fine," she said. "I just need to clear my head. I'm going for a walk."

"Are you sure that's safe?"

"Yes."

"I'm coming with you."

"No," she whispered. "Go back to sleep."

"I can walk," he protested. "The good doctor even said, and I quote, that fresh air is good."

"I'm sure it is. But you've just had brain surgery."

"And you're having heart surgery in about four hours," he retorted. He got out of bed and dragged a T-shirt over his head. "I'm fine, really."

Convalescing or not, Cecily knew she wouldn't win this argument. "Okay." She quickly dressed in her shorts and T-shirt. "Let's go."

But as they tiptoed out of their bedroom and down the stairs, Cecily was surprised to see light beaming weakly across the floor. When she looked in the living room, Dasha was sprawled on the couch, thincomp in hand. "Hi," Cecily whispered. "We're going out for a walk."

Dasha, bless her, didn't seem fazed. "Good idea," she said. "The tide's low. I'll leave the door unlocked for you to come back in. I'll be up for a while yet." She held up the thincomp. "I'm just tendering my resignation to the primary school."

Cecily remembered how much Dr. Caron and Dasha were giving up, just to help them. "Dasha, I'm sorry."

She shook her head. "Don't be. I'm looking forward to getting a chance to see more of the universe outside Sidra Prime. Oh, while you're on the beach, keep an eye out for crested crabs. They're nocturnal and mildly venomous."

"Oh, shit."

"Nah. They have big crown-like bumps on their heads and glow in the dark, so you won't miss them. Really bright orange and yellow, and they don't burrow in the sand or anything like that. Just step around them and you'll be fine."

"Thanks for the warning," Jason said.

"And don't swim. It's not safe at night."

"We weren't planning on it," Cecily said.

Dasha smiled. "In that case, see you in a bit."

They were quiet for a few moments as they walked in the surf, just as Cecily imagined it when she visited the beach with Dasha. Cold water gently rose up against the sand, and she spotted a crested crab resting in the sand a few meters away. Dasha hadn't been exaggerating about their brightness or color. They could easily double as nightlights if they weren't venomous or didn't have their gigantic claws.

Mildly venomous, she reminded herself. Not that she wanted to find out what that meant.

"Are you nervous?" Jason asked, breaking their silence.

"About the surgery? No." As she watched it, the crested crab lifted itself up on its huge claws and scurried further away from them. "I'm actually more nervous about finding Rordan and returning to Kurkay-2."

"Anders?" Jason guessed.

"Yeah. I want to patch things up between us."

"He does, too," Jason said gently. "He really does care about you."

"And I'm sure he'll be delighted once I quit this business." They'd already talked about Anders what felt like endlessly; she didn't want to keep harping on about her brother. But there was something else she wanted to discuss with him, and as his hand tightened around hers, she was reminded of it.

Maybe it's the reason I can't sleep.

"What happens after all this is over?" she blurted. "With us? Are you going back to Anders and Valenna's homestead, or are you...?" The question lingered in the air.

"Or am I staying with you?" he finished for her.

She nodded.

"I'd like to stay with you," he said.

Her heart leapt so suddenly that for half a second, she thought it was going to conk out on her again. "Really?"

"I thought about this right before Dr. Caron put me under," he said. "I love you."

Cecily froze, scarcely noticing when a rogue wave splashed freezing water over her feet. "You do?"

He looked a little sheepish, his eyes glowing on night vision. "I thought I should've told you before Dr. Caron started tinkering with my brain. But I didn't, so I figured the next best time was now." His eyes searched her face. "I told you before that I think you're the smartest and most capable person I've ever met. I still believe that."

Cecily still couldn't move or speak, still processing that Jason loved her.

"Say something," Jason said.

"I love you, too," she whispered, her words barely audible over the water. "And that's why I was so worried about you going back to live with Anders and Valenna when I have a perfectly good ship if we want to live on there, or I could buy a place..."

"It doesn't matter," Jason said. "I just want to be with you."

"I don't want to go for heart surgery without telling you," Cecily said. "And I didn't know how because I've never said it to anyone before." She paused. "Except Anders. And obviously that isn't the same thing. And I'm babbling. I'm sorry."

Amusement laced his words. "Don't worry about it. This is new for me, too."

Before she could respond, he picked her up, holding her to his chest, and walked away from the water. Anticipation raced through her, and she kissed the spot under his ear where his pulse beat, warm and steady. He sucked in a harsh breath but didn't set her down on the sand.

"What is it?" she asked.

"The water's full of crested crabs," Jason said, turning around so she could see them. Her skin prickled when she saw the glowing creatures crawling up the sandbar, all in different directions.

"I guess beach sex is out of the question."

"There's always the sim chamber on the *Gray Ghost*," Jason said, pressing a kiss to her temple. "Let's go back to bed."

CHAPTER 14

CECILY EASED into the velvet-covered pilot's seat. It felt good to be back at the *Gray Ghost*'s controls. It felt good to know that she and Jason were healthy again; that Marshall and Dasha Caron were safe.

All we have to do next is find Rordan Alexander and everything will be perfect.

As she initiated a pre-flight systems check, another thought struck her. *And patch things up with Anders.* Then *everything will be perfect.*

Sidra Prime's transit control authorized the *Ghost*'s departure and Cecily started the engines. She activated the intraship comm: "Prepare for liftoff. Don't worry about strapping in."

Dr. Caron and Dasha appeared delighted with their luxuriously appointed cabins when she brought them aboard, with Dasha declaring that she never wanted to leave the *Gray Ghost*.

Catching Jason's eye from where he sat next to her, she smiled. His dark eyes glittered in response, and with that look, she felt a corresponding heat spread through her.

When the *Gray Ghost* had safely broken atmosphere and

was cruising in the lanes, she stood up. "Can you keep an eye on all of this for me?" she asked him.

"Of course. Is everything okay?"

"Yeah," she said. "I just want to send a message to Anders. He should know we're all right."

It hurt that he hadn't reached out to her since her last message, more than she expected. Now that the threat of her heart failing was behind her, that was all she could focus on.

Jason's expression softened. "Got it. I'll be right here."

Cecily thought about the letter she wrote to Anders before Jason restarted her heart, and wondered what she was going to say to him now that her survival was ensured. Once in her cabin, she closed the door and set up her thincomp to face her, then pinged his transmit address.

Just when she thought he was going to ignore her, his surprised face filled the screen. "Hi," he said. "Did you find Marshall Caron?"

Cecily nodded. "He's on board the ship. So is his daughter."

"What—why? And why have you been incommunicado for so long? We were getting worried!"

Cecily softened a little at hearing those words. "There's a lot to explain about that," she said. "And I'll do it when we get back to Kurkay-2, when we can be sure our conversation won't be hacked. But Jason and I had our surgeries and we're going to live. Where did you hide out?" She remembered her warning to him to get out.

"We stayed put."

"Why would you do that?" Outrage colored her words.

"Where would we go?" he said. "We hardly know anyone. We don't have a ship to take off. We have animals dependent on us. So, we stayed." His expression softened. "I don't want to fight, okay? We're all okay."

Anders was right, and she didn't want to argue with him,

not when she had bad news to deliver. Shame tinged her next words. "We still haven't found Rordan Alexander."

"Yeah, about Alexander."

Oh, no. Cecily felt sick.

"Serena's working on that," Jason said. "As much as she can in her condition, anyway."

Any relief Cecily felt over knowing he could still be alive immediately evaporated. "What condition? Did her nanobots fuck up?"

"No," Anders replied. "Not at all. She's pregnant, about six months along. She and Matthias didn't say anything for a while because—well, obvious reasons. They were worried at first."

Cecily stared at him, then blinked as the weight of his words finally sunk in.

"Serena's *pregnant*?"

"Yeah, Matthias said he's been throwing up more than she has." Anders smiled, but it quickly disappeared. "But seriously, she's having a rough go of it. When we spoke to them, they said they didn't know if it was because it's just going to be a difficult pregnancy or because of her cyborg status. They're managing as best they can in terms of medical care, but it turns out there's a short supply of doctors with experience in cybernetics." His expression softened. "I can't tell you how glad I am that you found Dr. Caron. Do you think he'd be willing to help?"

"I don't want to speak for him, but I don't see why not. I'll pass her transmit details along to him."

"I know she and Matthias will really appreciate that," Anders said. "They're so excited about the baby but scared shitless. More than new parents usually are."

"Do you think they'll keep up the freighter business?"

"I hope not," said Anders, surprising her. "They need to

get the hell out of the Zone. This is a better place to raise a family."

Cecily remembered the things she wanted to tell him when she'd returned to Kurkay-2, how worried she was about the impending corporate threat to cyborg technology. "It isn't just the war," she said. "There are other issues facing cybernetics, and that's why we have to find Alexander. It isn't only the kill switch in his head."

"Could you stop speaking in riddles? Be a little more specific?" he asked, exasperated. "Just give me a basic outline of what we could expect, trouble-wise."

"There's a corporate interest in cybernetic technology," Cecily replied. "I know this because I had to take care of a Scout ship that was sent after us. We spent a few days in subspace to avoid it, and when we got out, there was an incident."

"I'm going to assume you took care of the incident because you're still standing."

"I did, and it was the last incident I'll ever have to take care of," she said. "At least, I hope it is." The memory of Robert Winters's face splitting open through his broken helmet came to mind, and she forced it away. "But everyone involved in cybernetics has to get out of the Zone. I heard talk of the border being closed again, so Serena and Matthias, and Lukas and Cressida need to escape. I have documentation I can pass along when we get back, once I encrypt it."

Anders nodded. "Thank you for telling me."

Just like that, their easy conversation, the first one they'd had in years, stalled. Cecily looked away, unsure what to say next.

But Anders surprised her. "I'm really glad you're okay," he said. "I thought about sending you a message telling you how I felt, but I didn't know how you'd feel about that, and I didn't want to upset you or Jason when you were already stressed out, so I wanted to talk to you directly. And then I worried that I wouldn't see you again if something happened."

Hope surged in her.

"Your life the last few years hasn't been easy," he said. "I get that. And Valenna's been telling me I'm being way too hard on you."

Tears pushed at her eyes. "I miss you so much."

"I missed you, too," he said. "I want us to be friends again. I was worried sick the entire time you and Jason were away, and now that you've told me you had an *incident,* I'm even more worried because I know there's shit you aren't telling me."

"Yeah." She swiped at her eyes with her hand. "Um, my heart started failing when we were in subspace and Jason restarted it."

"What the *fuck*?" Shock had Anders's eyes wider than she'd ever seen them, and she couldn't keep herself from smiling at the sight.

"It's okay," she said. "I promise. He downloaded everything he could into his head about my condition and followed the sickbay comp's directions to reset it until I could have it replaced entirely. I'm still alive because of him."

"He saved you," Anders said, and he visibly relaxed.

"Yeah. In a lot of ways."

He lifted an eyebrow. "Is there something else you're not telling me?"

"You probably don't want me to tell you."

It took a few seconds for her subtext to sink in. "Oh, God," Anders said.

Cecily heard Valenna laugh in the background, and she did, too. "You know we're all adults, right?" Cecily said.

"I know, and I hope it works for you," Anders replied. "I really do. You're both good people."

Anders's approval of her relationship with Jason meant

more than she expected, and the knots of tension she'd been holding since Omega-Three-Omega finally dissolved. This was the first real, friendly conversation she and her brother had had in years, and it felt so good to have their old camaraderie back. It could only get better from there.

"We're coming back to your place for now," Cecily said. "We'll be there in a couple of days at the most, although we won't be bunking with you two. Dr. Caron and Dasha are already looking at properties to rent nearby, and Jason and I have to find a place."

"Why not stay on the *Gray Ghost*?"

"I'm tired of living on a ship," she said. "I'm ready to settle down and live in a house like a normal person, and Jason is, too. We want to have normal lives."

"I'm happy to hear that," Anders said. "And not the part about changing careers. I just hope you and Jason settle down near us."

"I'm not the farming type."

"There are some beautiful luxury apartment blocks not too far from here," he said. "About an hour away by flitter, less by shuttle or wheeler. You'd never have to deal with animal shit or mulching there. And those blocks aren't like the ones on Echo-7. They're actually really nice."

"Thank you for the suggestion," she said, meaning it. She'd love to have an apartment near her brother and Valenna.

Anders looked over his shoulder. "Speaking of animals, I have a goat that needs to be milked, and she only tolerates me doing it."

"That bitch kicked me twice last time I tried," Valenna called from somewhere in the room.

"Yeah, but she's otherwise adorable, and so is her kid," Anders said. To Cecily, he said, "I'll see you soon."

"Two days at the most."

"Stay out of trouble."

"I will. I promise."

"I love you, Cecily," he said.

Another lump formed in her throat. "I love you, too."

Cecily let Jason land the *Gray Ghost* close to Anders and Valenna's home. A light rain misted across the landscape, and a pair of twin rainbows arched over their house, sights Jason hadn't realized how much he'd missed until now.

He, Cecily, Dr. Caron, and Dasha made the short walk to the house, bags and duffels loaded on an antigrav pallet behind them. Dr. Caron happily chattered about the new chapter in his life while Dasha took in their verdant surroundings.

Valenna was waiting by the house's gate when they walked up the drive, a blue rain hat covering her dark braided hair and mesh bag of gorkian leaves in her hand. She tossed the bag aside when she saw them and opened the gate, arms held out to hug him, and then Cecily. "I'm so glad you're all back in one piece," she said. Turning around, she yelled, "*Anders!*" back at the house, which was a hundred meters away from the gate. To them, she said, "He'll hear me. Cybernetic ears."

"And underwater breathing abilities, I hear," said Dr. Caron. He held out his hand to her. "Marshall Caron."

"From Caron Cybernetics," Valenna said, shaking it. "Valenna Merchant, Lukas Best's sister-in-law."

"I doubt Mr. Best has a great deal of good things to say about me," Dr. Caron said.

"We'll find out soon enough," Valenna replied. "Our friend Matthias is out in the Zone now, evacuating him and my sister before hell breaks loose again."

Some of Dr. Caron's joviality evaporated.

"If it's any consolation, Lukas was angrier with his father

than you," said Valenna, trying to smooth over the conversation. "He's never mentioned you specifically."

Dr. Caron didn't look convinced. "I know my research was misused," he said. "I'm trying to atone for that now, in the small ways I'm able." He gestured to Dasha, who lingered behind the rest of them. "This is my daughter, Dasha."

Valenna stuck out her hand. "Nice to meet you."

Anders was now approaching them, followed by Serena Glazer, who moved more slowly than Jason remembered. When they joined the group, he saw how pronounced her baby bump was, as well as the dark half-moons under her eyes.

"I guess congratulations are in order," Jason said to her by way of greeting.

"I appreciate them," Serena replied. "Even if I can't keep anything down right now." To Dr. Caron, she said, "Please tell me you're the doctor."

"I am," he said, beaming. "You must be Ms. Glazer."

"The one and only female cyborg with deactivated nanobots," she said. "And six months pregnant and I haven't seen a doctor yet."

"We'll do something about that right away."

"Oh, thank God," she said. "Matthias and I have been making do with the sickbay on his ship, but it's not the same. It keeps saying everything's okay, but I have all these nanobots in me, and..." Her face crumpled and tears leaked from her eyes. "He's picking up Lukas and Cressida right now, and I can't stop crying, and we both really want this baby, but we were so surprised about it." A sob escaped her, and Valenna wrapped her arms around her in a hug. "I don't even know for sure if my baby will be normal!" she wailed into Valenna's shoulder.

"There's a sickbay on the *Ghost*," said Dr. Caron kindly. "If it's any consolation to you, I've delivered a few babies in my time, and occasionally in much less ideal conditions than what we have here."

"Can you do it now?" asked Serena, pulling away from Valenna. She scrubbed her hand across her eyes. "I don't want to impose, but I just need to know for sure that the baby and I are both healthy."

"Of course. That won't be a hardship at all."

"I'll get our flitter to take you back to the ship," said Valenna. A goat wandered into the yard, saw Valenna, and charged. "Shit!" she yelped and bolted. "Anders, she's doing it again!"

The goat chased Valenna away, and both disappeared behind the house to the barn.

"You didn't do anything," Cecily said to Anders.

"Dolly will give up as soon as she sees her baby at the back of the house," Anders said. "As long as Valenna isn't trying to milk her or pet her or anything, she'll leave her alone. And Dolly hates the flitter."

Valenna returned a few moments later on the flitter, minus the goat. Dr. Caron helped Serena into it, then climbed in beside her. "We can get on your ship?" she asked Cecily.

Cecily nodded. "Your palm's authorized for the exterior lock."

"Thank you. We'll be back in a while," Valenna said to the rest of the group, and the flitter took off.

"Well, let me take you to the house," Anders said. Cecily and Dasha walked ahead, the antigrav pallet alongside them, while Jason and Anders lingered behind.

"Cecily told me," Anders said, voice low. "About you two."

"Yeah, she mentioned that." Jason suddenly felt nervous. "Is that going to be okay?"

"I want things to work out for you," Anders replied. "I'd like to have you in the family." He paused. "Well, we're already family. Being trapped on a planet by a psychopath will do that to people."

Jason nodded.

"But seriously, Formosa, if you break her heart, I'll end you." Anders clapped him on the back.

Jason smiled. "I wouldn't dream of it. I love her."

"Does she know that?"

"Yeah."

"Good."

Side by side, they walked back to the house.

ABOUT THE AUTHOR

Jessica Marting is a sci-fi and paranormal romance author, art enthusiast (not quite an artist, despite all that time in art school), an avid reader, and makeup collector. She lives in Toronto.

Sign up for her newsletter at jessicamarting.com/newsletter for pre-order alerts, sales, freebies, and more.

ALSO BY JESSICA MARTING

Magic & Mechanicals

Wolf's Lady

Sea Change

Bound in Blood

Dragon's Keep

Zone Cyborgs

Haven

Paradise

Oasis

Safe Harbor

Sanctuary

Refuge

The Commons

Supernova

Celestial Chaos

Standalone Novels & Novellas

Spindle's End

Trade Secrets

Neon Vice

Dead Ringer

Escape From Europa 10

Castaways
Demon's Favor

www.ingramcontent.com/pod-product-compliance
Lightning Source LLC
Chambersburg PA
CBHW031000210726
48290CB00007B/2398